SYDNEY MACKENZIE KNOCKS 'EM DEAD

SYDNEY MACKENZIE KNOCKS 'EM DEAD

CINDY CALLAGHAN

Aladdin

New York   London   Toronto   Sydney   New Delhi

This book is a work of fiction. Any references to historical events, real people, or real places are used fictitiously. Other names, characters, places, and events are products of the author's imagination, and any resemblance to actual events or places or persons, living or dead, is entirely coincidental.

ALADDIN

An imprint of Simon & Schuster Children's Publishing Division

1230 Avenue of the Americas, New York, New York 10020

First Aladdin paperback edition March 2018

Text copyright © 2017 by Cindy Callaghan

Cover illustration copyright © 2017 by Dung Ho Hahn

Also available in an Aladdin hardcover edition.

All rights reserved, including the right of reproduction in whole or in part in any form.

ALADDIN and related logo are registered trademarks of Simon & Schuster, Inc.

For information about special discounts for bulk purchases, please contact Simon & Schuster Special Sales at 1-866-506-1949 or business@simonandschuster.com.

The Simon & Schuster Speakers Bureau can bring authors to your live event.

For more information or to book an event, contact the Simon & Schuster Speakers Bureau at 1-866-248-3049 or visit our website at www.simonspeakers.com.

Cover designed by Jessica Handelman

Interior designed by Mike Rosamilia

The text of this book was set in Centaur MT.

Manufactured in the United States of America 0218 OFF

2 4 6 8 10 9 7 5 3 1

Library of Congress Cataloging-in-Publication Data

Names: Callaghan, Cindy, author.

Title: Sydney Mackenzie knocks 'em dead / by Cindy Callaghan.

Other titles: Sydney Mackenzie knocks them dead

Description: First Aladdin hardcover edition. | New York : Aladdin, 2017. |

Summary: "West Coast girl Sydney Mackenzie moves to Delaware after her parents inherit a cemetery—and becomes involved in a mystery surrounding the Underground Railroad. Will Sydney's filmmaking skills and the help of some new friends be enough for her get to the bottom of the mystery of her new home?"— Provided by publisher.

Identifiers: LCCN 2016036541 | ISBN 9781481465694 (hc) | ISBN 9781481465687 (pbk)

LCCN 2016036541

Subjects: | CYAC: Moving, Household—Fiction. | Cemeteries—Fiction. | Friendship—Fiction. | Mystery and detective stories.

Classification: LCC PZ7.C12926 Sy 2017 | DDC [Fic] —dc23

LC record available at https://lccn.loc.gov/2016036541

ISBN 9781481465700 (eBook)

TO JULIE, CHRIS, AND PAM.
In this book Sydney Mackenzie finds
her lifelong pals. It seems suitable to
dedicate this to my oldest Magoos with
heartfelt thanks for the many years
of froyo and high jinks.

The best way to predict the future is to create it.

—Abraham Lincoln

chapter one

LIFE ON THE SUNNY SIDE

EVEN THOUGH I HATED VAMPIRES AND JUST about anything scary, I'd seen *Fangs for You* five times.

"I loved it more than last week," my best friend, Leigh, said.

"Me too—Emiline was amazing," I agreed. "Totally amazing!" I dreamed of being exactly like fifteen-year-old Hollywood sweetheart Emiline Hunt someday. Someday soon. I could see it now: I walk down the red carpet, blinded by camera flashes. My name is in big, bright lights—*Fangs for Me*: Starring Sydney Mackenzie.

Back in the real world, Leigh and I pushed open the tinted-glass door of the Regal Cinema LA.

"So what now?" Leigh asked.

"You know what would make this day even more perfect? If we went for some froyo!"

"Yes!" Leigh said. "*That* is a fab idea."

We walked to Christina's Frogurt, our favorite place for fab froyo. Christina's had *the* best flavors, including California Colada, Leigh's fave, and Satiny Red Velvet Cake, my ultimate. As we walked, I checked my phone for messages.

That's when the unthinkable happened. A kid on a skateboard bumped into me and knocked it out of my hand. In slow motion it fell to the ground, crashed, bounced, and landed in three pieces.

[Pause for dramatic effect.]

"Sorry," he called as he boarded away. But sorry wasn't going to help. I'd spent months secretly cat-sitting to earn enough money for that phone.

"No biggie," Leigh said. Of course it wasn't a biggie to Leigh. She had her dad's gold Amex for "emergencies." I carried around my mom's expired card for show. "We'll go to the Apple Store after this and get you a new one."

"That's okay," I said. "I want the new one that isn't out yet. I totally have to have it."

"Oh yeah. Me too," she said. "But what will you use until then?"

I held the three pieces. "This doesn't look bad. Jim can probably fix it." Jim is my dad, and he is the most unhandy person in the world.

"If he can't, I think I have my old one in a drawer somewhere. You can totally have it." Leigh always shared her stuff with me.

We got our yogurt and ate at an outside table.

Leigh forgot about my phone, but I worried that without it I'd be a social outcast, which was something I couldn't afford.

Wearing big hide-my-face-because-I'm-ultra-popular-and-don't-want-to-be-recognized sunglasses, we pored over the latest issue of *Teen Dream* magazine, the one with Emiline Hunt on the cover.

Leigh pointed to a dress. "Your strappy Guess sandals would look good with that."

"Totally." The sandals weren't actually Guess. Leigh had assumed they were, and I didn't correct her.

I glanced at my watch. "I have to get home. My yoga instructor is coming to the house at five." It was really Roz's (aka my mom's) yoga instructor, who I pretended was mine, and he wasn't coming today. I actually had to check on the neighborhood cats. Things had changed for my family as business at our sporting goods stores slowed down: I started a secret cat-sitting business and lied to keep up appearances with Leigh, while Jim let the country club membership go and skipped a weekender in Baja with his friends. But Roz had more trouble acclimating to the Mackenzies' new financial status. In fact, she *hadn't* acclimated. "Things will turn around," she kept saying.

"I thought yoga was Wednesdays," Leigh said.

I dotted gloss onto my lips. "I needed an extra session this week. You know, to relax."

"I get that. Eighth grade is totally high pressure."

"So high," I agreed, untangling myself from my web of lies. I grabbed a bus home with no idea that my parents were about to drop a bomb that would destroy my sunny, silver-screeny, thrilling, froyo, medium-popular world in Southern California.

chapter two

THE PLAN TO RUIN MY LIFE

I'M NOT ONE TO EXAGGERATE, BUT MY PARENTS decided to ruin my life. It started right after the yogurt.

"Roz! I'm home, and I have a serious problem."

What if someone was trying to text me right now?

I did a double take when I saw my parents, Roz and Jim Mackenzie, hanging out in the living room when Jim should've been at one of the stores, and Roz should have been at Pilates.

Roz sat on the light-tan leather couch, her hands in tight fists in her lap, while Jim paced across the Oriental rug, back and forth in front of the piano that no one played.

Was I in trouble?

I recalled the recent torture I'd inflicted on my twin six-year-old brothers. I didn't think it was bad enough to result in a lecture from both Roz *and* Jim.

"We have to talk to you," Roz said. "Sit down."

Jim's forehead wrinkled. "We've sold the sporting goods stores."

"Okay. Why?" I asked.

"We were losing money. In fact, we lost a lot of money."

I figured we couldn't afford to lose a lot of money.

"We're going to make some changes." Roz's voice cracked around "changes."

"Like what?" Was I going to be phoneless or homeless?

"Some very difficult, very big changes." Her tone told me we were heading toward homeless.

"We're thinking about this family's future," Jim said. "We need to make more money, and spend less—a lot less." He looked at Roz when he said that last part.

Roz made an effort to mutter, "And *save* more."

Jim's expression lightened, and he began to look more like the glass-is-half-full kinda guy I knew. "So, we're starting a new business! One that booms regardless of the economy."

"A yogurt boutique?" I started dreaming of all the

free taste testing Leigh and I would get to do. "Can I pick the flavors and design the T-shirts?"

They shook their heads.

"People aren't always going to buy expensive clothes or go out to eat," Jim explained. "We want a business that's 'recession proof.'" He made air quotes with his fingers.

"What's 'recession proof'?" I mimicked his quotes.

"You see, Sydney," Roz began. "As sad as it is, people are always going to die. And they need a place . . . er . . . what I mean is, they need to go to a—"

Jim jumped in. "What your mother is trying to say is that we've inherited a cemetery. That's going to be our new family business." Jim grinned widely. This man could find the best in any terrible situation, but come on, *a cemetery*?

"A what?" I tugged on my ears. "These must not be working, because I think you just said 'cemetery.'" Then I turned to look over each of my shoulders for a hidden camera. "Wait. This is a joke, right? Is this for a viral video contest? Good one. You got me for a minute. What do I win?"

"Syd, it's not a joke," Roz said. "There's no contest."

"A cemetery," Jim repeated.

My mouth hung open as I waited for him to fill in the blanks.

"Yes, ma'am." Jim smacked his hands together. "People will always have a consistent need for cemetery services. It's brilliant!" He put his arm around Roz's shoulders. "Isn't that right?"

"Uh-huh." Roz forced a smile that I suspected covered a good cry. "Your father's uncle Ted—"

Jim interrupted. "Theodore Mackenzie the Fifth."

"That's right. The fifth in a long line of Mackenzie men. Well, Uncle Teddy owned a cemetery. And sadly, he recently died."

"Bummer. Did, um, I ever meet this Uncle Ted the Fifth?"

"We weren't close to him," Jim said. "But since he had no children, he left the business to me. To US! And the timing couldn't be more perfect." He rubbed his hands together. "Perfect timing for *big* changes for the Mackenzies."

"That's right," Roz chimed in much less convincingly.

"Yup," Jim said. "It's the perfect time to change businesses and move. To Delaware."

I lifted my hand. "Hold up. Delaware?"

Roz and Jim nodded and smiled, one more enthusiastically than the other.

"Really? Where is Delaware? You're not serious? Like, the kind of cemetery with dead people?"

I didn't ask what was probably the most important question of all: *Can I get a new phone?*

Jim answered:

"Really.

"East Coast.

"Totally serious.

"Don't think there is any other kind.

"And there's more," Jim said. "We're going to drive across country, all of us together in the car for five days." When Jim said "all of us," he was including my brothers. "Talk about quality family time. It doesn't get much better than that!"

Ugh!

Once I was convinced that they did, in fact, intend to ruin my life, I ran to my room and slammed the door.

I called Leigh on the regular old-fashioned cordless phone.

She answered, "Talk to me, Syd."

"My life is over," I said. "Over. *Finito. Fini.*"

"Again?"

"This time it really is."

"Why?" she asked.

"Are you sitting down?"

I heard a shuffle. "I am now. Whatcha got?"

I said, "I'm moving."

"Out of Orange County?"

"Yup."

"To where? San Diego? San Fernando? Puh-lease don't say San Francisco."

"Worse."

"Sacramento?" she asked.

"Delaware."

"I've never heard of it," Leigh said. "Is it near Palo Alto?"

"The STATE! It's all the way over on the other side of the country."

"Eeewww. Why? Do Roz and Jim hate you?"

"I think so," I said. "I have a map. It's next to New Jersey. I looked it up."

"Doesn't New Jersey smell like armpits?"

"I hope not," I said. "But thanks, that's very helpful."

"You're right. Your life *is* over. Why are they doing this to you, Magoo?" Leigh and I called everything Magoo. It came from a teacher we had once. She called Leigh a Chatty Magoo, which she so totally is, but still, that was a super-dorky thing to say. Now it was like "our word," and we used it all the time.

I explained about the sporting goods stores, the economy, recessions, Uncle Ted, and the inheritance.

"A cemetery?" Leigh made gagging sounds. "I'm so not visiting you."

"Why not?"

"Because it's majorly Creepy Magoo." Then she asked, "What are you gonna do?"

"I don't know yet. Can I live with you?"

"Umm, I don't think so, Syd. My mom is nuts."

"Hmm . . ." She had a point.

"Are they leaving the Dumb-Os behind?" She meant my twin brothers. "That would be good, right?"

"I'm pretty sure they're coming with us," I said.

chapter three

THE PLAN TO REPAIR MY LIFE

THE NEXT DAY LEIGH'S MOM DROPPED US OFF AT Orange County Junior High in her red Porsche. We fit right in among the fancy cars in the carpool lane. I could pretend to have a lot of name-brand things, but it was hard to make up an expensive sports car. Jim used to have one, but he traded it in for a "certified pre-owned" Jeep, which was still pretty cool because you could take the top down.

I was really bummed from the news Roz and Jim had laid on me last night. I couldn't sleep, so I had gotten up extra early and done my hair. Every strand was perfect. The wind from the Porsche hadn't been kind to it, so I carefully finger-combed the new, long blond highlights back into place. "Does my hair look okay?" I'd told Leigh that I had gotten it done in Hollywood, but I did it myself from a kit I got at the drugstore. Turns out I'm pretty good at drugstore hair coloring.

"It looks great, Syd," Leigh said without looking away from her compact mirror while she walked.

That's when Gigi Greggory walked passed us. She swept her glossy locks over her shoulder. Her feet moved, but she walked so gracefully that she practically floated. "Hey," she said to us. "I like your hair, Sydney."

"Thanks." And that was why she was Gigi. She knew everybody's name, and she always had something nice to say. Gigi joined up with a group of mega-popular girls, none of whom were as nice or as pretty. Actually, most of them weren't nice at all.

I wanted to be popular like Gigi. Leigh and I were several rungs lower on the social ladder and always trying to climb higher; Leigh was faster than me. That's why we were on-again, off-again BFFs, because sometimes she was too far ahead for me to catch up. Right now we were on again. I figured that was because I'd gotten a part in this year's school production, *Romeo and Juliet*. It was a small, but impressive role and probably an indication of not only my future success at OCJH, but also in Hollywood.

Leigh said, "Lucky you. Gigi noticed your hair."

"I guess." "Lucky" wasn't the word I'd use to describe myself today. I opened my locker and got the books I needed for film history and drama. The rest of the day was filled with other classes that someone, somewhere, must've thought were important.

Leigh said, "I have math. What am I ever going to need math for? Isn't that why God made calculators?"

"Look on the bright side," I said. "There's chicken Caesar and tiramisu for lunch today."

"If I survive math, I'll meet you in the caf later," Leigh said.

"Gotcha," I said.

I slammed my locker, and we went our separate ways. I reached into my purse for my cell phone for something to stare at while I walked. It wasn't there, so I stared at the floor.

The fact was that I needed a new phone really, really badly. I didn't think Roz and Jim would sympathize with the social implications of my situation and fund a replacement.

Leigh and I sat at a corner table for lunch. She took out a Sharpie marker. "Okay, things we're going to do before you move to Delaware." She stuck a gag finger in her mouth when she said Delaware. The pukey jokes about Delaware weren't funny anymore.

"Cali Colada froyo . . ." She wrote on a napkin.

"I want to get some California Cannoli to freeze and take with me," I said.

"Good idea." She wrote it down. "Tomorrow, let's get some California rolls and sushi, because they probably don't have that in Creepsville," Leigh suggested.

"I'm sure they have sushi somewhere in the state," I said.

"Maybe," Leigh said. "But this is cooler because it's here. California is the common denominator in what's cool."

"Did you learn about denominators in math today?"

We giggled. Then I smacked Leigh on the arm, harder than I meant to, because I suddenly got *very* excited with a HUGE idea. "You just gave me an idea about Delaware!"

"I did?" she asked.

"Yeah. Here it is: I'm from *California.*"

"So what?" she asked.

"*That's* the silver lining in moving to Creepsville," I said.

She wasn't following.

"I'm tan, I've seen movie stars, I have great hair according to Gigi Greggory—"

"I don't think she said 'great.'"

I ignored her. "I surf."

"You *try* to surf."

I ignored that, too. "See what I'm trying to say?"

"Nope. Not even a little."

"California is the common denominator in c-o-o-l. That's why all the celebs are here. These Delaware peeps will think I'm totally *California* cool. Plus, I have great clothes," I added. "Nobody there knows where I rank on the Orange County Junior High food chain. I can be whoever I want there. I can be *their Gigi*."

We spent the rest of lunch working on a plan for me to be the most popular kid at my new school. When we finished it, I neatly folded the napkins we'd written on and put them in my backpack.

I said, "Leigh, I'm going to miss you so much. Will you visit me?"

"I'll miss you too, and I'd text you all the time, but since you don't have a cell phone, I guess we could e-mail sometimes," she said. "Don't know if I'll visit the *East* Coast, if you know what I mean."

My face fell.

Leigh must've noticed. "No offense. It's all the cold, and dead stuff. There are probably all kinds of ghosts hanging around there. It's not personal. I hope you'll come back here and visit me."

"Sure, Leigh," I said, but I'd stopped listening around "dead stuff" and focused on my plan for Gigi-esque status at my new school.

chapter four

THE SCENERY FOR MY NEW LIFE

JIM'S JEEP DROVE EAST ON THE INTERSTATE. THE trees had fewer leaves every hour. It had been an unpleasant trip, like, the worst. Roz chatted about how this change would bring us all closer together, and how getting away from the California scene would be a good change. I didn't believe a word of it. I don't think she did either.

Since leaving our last pit stop in Maryland, the twins, Dumb-O One and Dumb-O Two, had watched nothing but Christmas DVDs and sung carols loudly. I was going totally bonkers without my phone—the itch to text and play with my apps was driving me crazy. And if I heard "Frosty" one more time, I was gonna melt that sucker myself.

I shoved earbuds in deep, shuffled a playlist, and

tuned them out to focus on my popularity plan, which I named the S5. It stood for Sydney's Super Social Stardom Schedule. I'd started it days before we left, and I finished it when we entered Colorado.

It was a simple plan, really.

THE S5
1. HAVE AN AWESOME LOOK: CLOTHES,
   HAIR, ETC. . . .
2. MAKE SURE EVERYONE KNOWS
   I'M FROM CALIFORNIA AND THAT
   CALIFORNIA ROCKS
3. BE NICE TO EVERYONE
4. STAR IN THE SCHOOL PLAYS
5. MOST IMPORTANT: DON'T LET ANYONE
   KNOW ABOUT THE CEMETERY THING

I closed my eyes, and in my head I played scenes like a movie preview, with bouncy music in the background.

Scene:

I walk into the cafeteria in my awesome dark purple tank top and white skirt. My legs are tan. Everyone waves me over to sit at their table. Since

I can't choose, I sit at an open table and invite everyone to come eat with me. They do.

My bangle bracelets knock together as I stir my iced caramel latte with a swizzle straw. The girls love my hair slightly spritzed with glitter, which I share with them.

The most popular, cutest boy in eighth grade, who all the girls love, invites me to the movies. The girls are jealous, but they can't hate me, because I'm so nice. They beg me to act out a scene from MAXINE THE MARVELOUS, and I do. The drama teacher, who happens to be in the caf, sees my performance and asks me to take the lead in the next school production. The kids tell me that I just have to do it, so I accept.

After days of quality family time, I saw the sign WELCOME TO BUTTERMILK RIVER COVE, DELAWARE—POPULATION 800.

The streets of Buttermilk River Cove were quiet, the houses small, run-down, and close together. Dirty snow piles lined the roads like mud mountains. Christmas lights, the kind with real big bulbs, not little white twinkly ones, were lit, even though it wasn't dark yet and Christmas was weeks ago. My excitement over my new life fizzled at the sad appearance of the town. If you thought of California as bright lights, brilliant colors, sunshine, and flashing cameras, Buttermilk River Cove was dull, dark, and depressed.

Roz fidgeted in her seat. "Turn here, Jim."

After going down one street and making a turn, it seemed like we'd gone through the entire town.

"Oh my," Roz said at the sight of the house. "It doesn't look quite like the picture, does it?"

Jim didn't seem to hear. "There she is. The Victorian. Built in 1830. Uncle Ted's lawyer sent me the entire history of the place. It's fascinating."

At this sight any bouncy music emerging from my scene stopped.

Oh dark and spooky Magoo.

"That's the house we're going to live in?" I asked.

It was the biggest house I'd seen in Buttermilk River Cove. Its white and navy paint peeled; the shutters were crooked; the roof sagged. It kind of leaned to the right like it was tired of standing for the last hundred and eighty years or so.

On either side of the house was a black wrought-iron fence surrounded by tall, angry-looking dead weeds. Over a gated entrance, metal letters said:

LAY TO REST CEMETERY

A PLACE TO SPEND ETERNITY

ESTABLISHED 1602

Jim drove the Jeep into the half-moon-shaped driveway and pulled up next to the house. Our headlights shone on the backyard.

I could not believe what I saw.

"You've. Got. To. Be. Kidding. Me."

Goose bumps covered every inch of my tan skin.

"What?" Roz said.

"Those are tombstones!" I yelled.

"Of course they're tombstones. It's a cemetery," Jim said.

"You left out an important detail." I felt deceived. "You failed to mention that the graveyard was in OUR BACKYARD!" I shivered. There was no way I was getting out of this car.

The Dumb-Os climbed over the backseat, kicking me in the head on their way out the door.

"Cool!" One yelled.

"Awesome!" Two yelled.

How could these twerps not be scared?

Jim got out. "The best way to run a business is to be at it all the time. That was a mistake I made with the sporting goods stores. I trusted other people to manage the day to day. I'm not going to do that again. The cemetery office is on the first floor of the house. We'll live upstairs. It'll be perfect."

It was the opposite of perfect.

If you could take perfect and turn it upside down and run it over with a Porsche, then shove it in a NutriBullet, you might be getting close to how far we were from perfect.

I stayed in the dark car. I couldn't believe it. Just like that, my dream of being the Buttermilk River Cove Gigi was destroyed. Gone. Blown away. Disintegrated.

I was going to be the weird kid.

The one who lived in a cemetery.

How could I possibly hide a bazillion tombstones . . . in my *backyard*? It wasn't like hiding an extra toe, or a peanut allergy, or two pain-in-the-butt twin brothers, or the brand of my shoes.

My fate was sealed: I was going to be the Freaky Magoo of Buttermilk River Cove.

[Gloomy music plays in the background.]

When I realized I was in the car all alone, I reluctantly set a foot on the frozen ground, sending a chill up my back.

Jim walked up the Victorian's front steps. They creaked. I followed, every cell of my body stuffed with fear. Jim opened the door and disappeared across the threshold. He turned on a chandelier, which barely lighted the foyer enough for us to see the faded, frayed braided rug and thick, peeling wallpaper.

"Get your bags, boys," Jim called to One and Two. To Roz and me he said, "The movers confirmed all our stuff is here. Let's go up and check it out."

I grabbed Roz's arm. She held mine, too, offering me a smidgen of comfort.

"Jim, can you find a few more lights?" she asked.

Jim flicked one switch then another, having little luck. "First thing tomorrow we've gotta replace some bulbs."

"Hundred watts," Roz suggested.

Jim didn't hear her because he'd climbed up the curved staircase. "Ouuch!" he yelled.

Roz clenched my arm tighter. "What happened?"

"I bumped my head. I'm fine." A dim light came on. "Ah. There we are. Our furniture looks good. It looks just like home. Come on up."

Roz called the twins again. I ascended the winding stairs and examined the first room, a living room. Seeing our furniture relaxed me a little, but if Jim thought this looked like home, he needed a sip of

Reality Juice. It was here but covered by brown cardboard packing boxes filled with stuff and the distinct smell of yuck.

Roz dropped heavy bags from her shoulders. "Ah, home," she said, flopping onto the couch. She popped right back up. "It's wet! The couch is wet!"

I extended my hand to touch a mysterious spot. I looked up. "Jim, I think there's a leak in the roof."

He came over. "Don't call me Jim. Regular kids don't call their parents by their first names."

"I live in a cemetery," I said. "I don't think I qualify as a regular kid."

With one hand on his hip and the other over my shoulder, he asked calmly, "Just call me Dad?" He looked up. "Yup. Looks like a leak. Old houses have leaks." Removing his hand, he touched the wall. "Yup, they don't build 'em like this anymore." He knocked on the wall and a chunk of withered wallpaper crackled off the wall, but his smile remained.

Maybe they didn't make 'em like this anymore on purpose.

"I'll work on it tomorrow." He walked around the room rubbing his hands together. "A coat of paint, a little buff on these beautiful hardwood floors, some new fixtures, and this place is going to be a beaut.

Houses this old don't exist in California. Nope. You find architecture like this in the First State. You know this house is on the National Historic Register? I love it already. THANK YOU, UNCLE TEDDY!" He stood next to me, hand back on hip, the other around my back, admiring the craftsmanship of the house.

Roz reappeared with a pot, which she placed under the leak. "Might need more than a coat of paint," she said.

"Yup. Big plans. I'm going to convert the basement into an awesome game room." At that comment the lights flickered. He ignored it. "They used to use that space for mortuary stuff, but not anymore. Funeral homes do that now, so sky's the limit down there. You're gonna love it! Maybe a space for yoga, too?" he asked Roz.

She didn't answer him. The look on her face said she didn't love the house as much as Jim. She stood on the other side of me, with an arm over my shoulder. I was sandwiched between them.

A breeze of icy air floated through the room. "Is there a window open?" I asked.

"Hmm?" Jim asked. "What do you mean?"

"Don't you feel that cold air?"

"I like it," Jim said. "Brisk."

Apparently I was the only one covered with goose bumps.

"The heat will kick in soon," Jim said. "This is going to be a Great Mackenzie Adventure. We're going to look back at this very moment some day and say, 'Remember what the Victorian looked like that first night?'"

"Uh-huh," said Roz.

The Dumb-Os barreled into the living room howling like ghosts, messing up this picture-perfect parental moment.

That night I crawled into my bed and blocked thoughts of my freezing toes and nose, the smell of mildew, and the field of dead people buried on the other side of my bedroom wall by playing a mental movie preview.

Scene:

> *I walk into homeroom and look to the teacher for my seat. "Oh, you're the folks who live at Lay to Rest?" she asks. I nod. The kids' faces register shock and disgust. They whisper and point. I take my seat, and the kids on either side of me slowly slide their chairs away. One of the kids says, "She*

smells like a corpse." No one even gets to know my name, except maybe the chubby boy eating boogers.

I pulled the pillow over my head.

Then Jim came in. "Good night, honey. I turned the heat up. It'll just take a little while to warm the whole house."

"Okay." My teeth chattered.

"I know you didn't want to move away from California and your friends, but you'll see, Syd, this is going to be great." I think he really believed that.

"Yup."

"Maybe losing the stores was a blessing in disguise," he continued.

I wasn't buying it. "Uh-huh."

"And we want you to help out around here more—with your brothers, the house, and the business. You didn't have any chores in California. Most kids have jobs around the house. You're going to have chores."

For a salesman, he wasn't doing a great job selling me on this. "Chores?"

"Yeah. Maybe I can even teach you a few things as we renovate the basement." The lights flickered again. "You can be my apprentice. And in exchange, you'll get an allowance to spend on whatever you want. After a few weeks, you'll get used to it. You'll see." He winked at me. "I'll see you in the morning, sweetheart." He blew me a kiss.

The Buttermilk River Cove breeze blew tree branches. The house moaned to resist the wind. There was a *thud!*

I sat up.

A thud?

It was definitely a thud.

I listened.

Nothing.

I pulled the covers over me and closed my eyes, imagining the gentle lap of the Pacific Ocean and the shiny banister of the escalator at the Galleria, when I heard another *thud!*

There was a howl of more wind, a hoot of an owl, a bark of a dog in the distance, a squeak, a groan, then sort of a sigh.

I knew what it was.

A thud, a groan, and a sigh?

It was a ghost.

[Horror movie music softly plays in the background.]

We had inherited a haunted cemetery in Delaware.

Gee, thanks, Great-uncle Teddy!

chapter five

MEETING THE CREW

WHAT I'D THOUGHT WAS A SPOOKY OLD haunted house in the middle of a cemetery at night was still a spooky old haunted house in the middle of a cemetery during the day.

It was overcast, cloudy, and cold. I found a box of my clothes and pulled on not one, but two pairs of hot-pink socks. I finger-combed my hair, the hair that Gigi Greggory had liked, tossed it into a clip, and slid on a pair of Urban Outfitters jeans over the leggings I'd worn to bed, because the house was still too cold to take them off. I looked around the room for a silver lining but didn't see one. I looked out the window; there wasn't one there, either. You know what was there? Tombstones.

In the living room Roz was already busily working.

Her head was covered with a bandana, her arms protected by gardening gloves. She wore an apron over a Juicy sweat suit like she knew what she was doing, which she didn't, because we'd always had a cleaning person, even when the stores weren't doing well and she probably should have done it herself. She tried to swipe cobwebs from the corners of the ceiling but caused more dust to fall from the beams.

"So, it wasn't just a bad dream," I said.

"What?"

"We still live in a cemetery."

She grabbed my shoulders and looked me in the eyes. "Where's your sense of adventure?"

"Roz, I get a weird feeling in this place. Don't you feel it?"

"It's just cold. You're not used to it."

"Did you hear those noises last night?"

"I didn't hear anything except the wind and the creaks of an old house," Roz said. "Give it a chance, okay?"

I guessed I could give it a wee little bit of a chance. And then a stinky droplet of water hit me on the nose.

"Where's Jim?" I asked. She gave me the *We've talked about this* look. "Where's *Dad*?"

"Downstairs meeting the staff." She snagged a web around her broom and held the sticky spiderness away from her like it was a snake.

"Staff?" I asked.

"Yes. Lay to Rest came with its former staff." She remained focused on the end of the broom, maybe trying to figure out what to do with the webs. "Dad is downstairs meeting them. Why don't you go and say hi?" I wondered if the staff would know if the cemetery was haunted. "And can you also bring me up a latte?"

I tilted my head and gave her a look that said, *We live in a cemetery—no lattes down there, Roz.*

"Fine," she said. "A hot tea?"

I nodded; that sounded possible.

"Oh, and later I want to talk to you about those chores."

I'm not a Chorey Magoo, but I said, "Sure. Where are One and Two?"

"They're playing outside. And they have names, Sydney."

The creaky steps of the Victorian were chilly even through two layers of socks.

Jim sat in the kitchen with two other people. He

was talking, but his voice was drowned out by a sound from a stainless-steel pitcher plugged into the wall. Brown bubbles popped in the pitcher's clear lid. I inspected it.

"It's a percolator," Jim said. "It makes coffee."

I looked more closely. "Can it make a decaf skinny mocha latte?" I wanted to wrap my hands around a warm cup. Maybe I'd crawl inside it.

"Sorry." Jim tossed me a hooded sweatshirt that had been hanging off the back of his chair. "Here, put this on. We'll have to look into getting some warmer clothes."

My ears perked up, because I'm pretty sure he just said we were going shopping. He saw my *I'm going shopping! I'm going shopping!* look. "Relax. Just a few no-nonsense sweatshirts."

The woman at the table said, "There's an army-navy store at the bottom of the hill. You can get some wool socks there too.

Won't they itch?

"Sounds good." Then Jim said, "Sydney, this is the crew that runs things here at Lay to Rest." He indicated the grandma-aged woman who looked like she'd been up for a major role in *Hocus Pocus*. "This is Joyce. She handles all the day-to-day office stuff."

Joyce was tall and thin. She had long, dark, straight hair streaked with gray. Her skin was so pale, it had a greenish tint. She wore a thick, knitted black shawl, and a long, heavy skirt that might've been made out of black tapestry.

"It's nice to meet you," I said.

Jim extended his arm toward the man standing cross-armed in the corner. "This is Mr. Corcoran." Mr. Corcoran was tall and thick, his hair military short. He had a scar that I tried not to stare at. It extended from one ear to mid skull. Mr. Corcoran wore coveralls over a red sweater that frayed at the neck and wrists. His socks were pulled up over the hem of his pants so that they were higher than his army-ish boots. He reminded me of *A Nightmare on Elm Street* meets *Frankenstein*. Jim said, "He is the um, the um . . ."

"Gravedigger," Mr. Corcoran interrupted. "Call me Cork. Everyone does." He didn't offer me his hand, but I noticed there was a lot of dirt under his nails. But I guess you'd expect a gravedigger to have grave dirt under his nails.

"Okay," I said. "Hi, Cork." If there was an audition for the part of Weird Gravedigger Guy, Cork wouldn't even have to read lines.

"They live in the quarters down here. Uncle Ted

had the back rooms renovated into apartments," Jim said. "They were just explaining the routine to me."

Joyce slid a chair from the table with her foot. "Why don't you have a seat, sweetheart?"

I thought about asking them about my haunting suspicions, but maybe not with Jim around.

"That's okay. I'm supposed to bring my mom tea, and then we're going to school to pick up my schedule for tomorrow."

"Okay," Jim said. "But before you do, would you please take this out back to the groundskeeper." He handed me a small gadget. "It's a pruner, for bushes."

I took the pruner, passed through a small workroom, slipped on a pair of Jim's boots, and went out a back door. It slammed behind me, making me jump. About twenty rows into the cemetery I saw a slender man. The two employees inside had taken the parts of Witch and Freddy Krueger. I wondered what was left for this guy: Mummy? Wolfman?

I cautiously stepped through the maze of headstones, freaked out to be stepping on dead people. I tried to stay on the tips of my toes and took the biggest steps I could. "Sorry," I whispered to the buried people. I hopped around a few. "Sorry, sorry. Sorry. Oh geez, I'm *really* sorry."

"Good morning," said the groundskeeper. He was younger than Joyce and Cork. He wore well-worn mid-calf Doc Martens, tight black jeans, a turtleneck wrapped in a checkerboard scarf, and a long black cloak. You don't see many cloaks around Hollywood. As unusual as that was, the style worked for him.

He reached out to shake, but his hand was palm down, almost like he wanted me to kiss it, which I didn't. His hand was cool and felt like a soggy noodle. "I'm Elliott, landscape designer."

"I'm Sydney, daughter of owner." I was close enough to suspect that he might've been wearing a splash of makeup—his thin lips were extra red, and his eyes stood out like they were enhanced with liner. If he was going for the vampire look, he was doing a good job.

He said, "Your dad told me you have plans this morning, but when you get back, I'm supposed to show you around because you're going to have a few jobs around here."

I said, "That sounds *greeaat*."

"Wait," Elliott said, "you don't sound like you mean that."

"I'm sorry," I apologized. "It's just that this is all a little new to me."

"I guess it's pretty different from LA." Then he said, "I hear your mom is taking you over to the school. It'll be a good opportunity to meet the other kids. Just tell them you live here and they'll love you."

Sure they will.

chapter six

CASTING CALL

ON THE WAY TO BUTTERMILK RIVER COVE Middle School, I cranked the heat in the Jeep, slicked gloss on my lips, and smoothed my hair that I'd flat-ironed.

"Roz, I think we're in the wrong place," I said when she stopped at the elementary school.

She double-checked the address and it was right.

In the office, Dr. Perkel, the principal, explained, "We consolidated and closed the middle school building."

"So this school goes from kindergarten to eighth grade?" I asked.

"That's right. It's economical."

I was going to be in the same school as the Dumb-Os. *Great.*

"My, how convenient," Roz said.

"I don't want to forget to tell you about our time capsule project. Everyone will add something, and we'll open it in twenty-five years. It's a big deal."

"Exciting." Roz tried to sound excited.

"And the cell phone policy. One word: none."

Roz said, "That won't be a problem, right, Syd?"

"None." . . . Because I didn't have a phone.

Then Dr. Perkel called a girl named Johanna Stevens to give me a tour. Meanwhile, Roz hung out in the office to sign papers.

While I waited for Johanna, I looked into the hallway to check out the kids. They were all different ages. I saw a lot of no-brand jeans, snow boots, bad hair, and pale skin.

Johanna came into the office. "So, you're the new girl?" She was petite and wore jeans that looked too big for her. I was glad I'd chosen jeans myself.

I made my best Gigi smile. "Yup, I'm the new girl." I followed Johanna down the hallway. It was lined with cubbies instead of lockers.

As I walked next to her, I could see that Johanna was not wearing any makeup, which made me self-conscious. When she wasn't looking, I blotted my lip gloss on the top of my hand and ran my finger over my eyelids to lessen the shadow.

"We don't get many new kids. I mean, we just don't get many people moving to Buttermilk River Cove. Maybe that's how come I know everyone. If you wanna know who someone is, you can just ask me. I guess not many people leave Buttermilk River Cove either. Maybe that makes sense, because if no one leaves, then there won't be any houses for new people to move into," Johanna said. "So, why did your family re-habitate?"

"Um, I think, um. Do you mean relocate?" I casually slid a jeweled clip out of my hair and buried it in my pocket.

"Yeah, that's what I meant, but I like to make up new words. Re-habitate has a nice sound to it." Johanna shuffled on the hallway floor in well-worn nylon boots that might've been good in the snow but weren't what I would call cute.

"My dad's uncle died, so we—"

"Oh my gosh! That is soooo sad. I am so so sorry. Was it sudden? Was it expected? Was he sick? He probably led a full life, you know." She tilted her head sympathetically. "And now he's in a better place."

"Right. Uh, thank you. I'm sure he is," I said.

"So, where do you live?" she asked.

According to the S5 plan I needed to avoid the

subject of Lay to Rest to secure a good position in the social ecosystem of Buttermilk River Cove Elementary/Middle School.

"Oh, in town," I said. Then quickly I added, "This is a nice school," which was a lie.

"Yeah. I've gone here since kindergarten. My parents went to school here too. We have a good hockey team, the Buttermilk River Cove Bulldogs. They won the state championship in 1974," she said. "Where did you say you li—"

"Is that the Delaware State Championships?"

"Right. Yeah. Delaware. That's the state we live in. It's the First State."

"So I've heard. That's great." And then I sprung the line that would launch me into social stardom: "I'm from California."

"You are? I guess it's tough to move away from your friends and stuff. But it's probably nice to get away from the earthquakes and gorillas. Maybe that's why people don't seem to move away from Buttermilk River Cove, because there are no earthquakes or gorillas. Where did you say you lived here, again?" Johanna asked.

Wait—what just happened? Johanna didn't care that I was from California. It must've been the way I said it.

"In town. In a house we inherited from my dad's uncle, the *dead* one." I hoped for more condolences, but she just continued to lead me down the dreary hallway. I asked, "So, hockey, huh? That's played on ice, right?"

"Right." She stopped walking and looked right at me. "Which house?"

I winced. It could no longer be avoided. "In the big Victorian on the top of the hill."

[Pause—the long, uncomfortable type.]

"Wait—you live at Lay to Rest? In the cemetery? In that old Victorian house? At the top of the hill? With those people who work there?" Johanna stared at me incredulously.

There it was.

My life was o-v-e-r.

I thought about saying *Just kidding* and making up something about living in a hotel until our new house was built, or living on the other side of town, but I didn't have enough information about this town to tell a good lie. I'd learned in California that the best way to pass as a rich, in-style, future movie star was to know a lot about rich people, style, and movies. But I didn't know enough to lie about Buttermilk River Cove. I wanted to say that I was a totally normal kid, worthy of being the most popular.

"Yup." I slumped. "That's the house." I waited for her to laugh in my face, cringe, maybe gag.

That's when the unexpected happened.

"THAT. IS. AWESOME!" Johanna squealed.

"It is?" I asked, confused.

"Oh yeah! In a big way. I love that old house. It's huge. My great-great-grandmother is buried there, so is my great-great-grandfather, my great-aunt Ellie, my great-grandmother and great-grandfather. I think everyone at this school has dead relatives buried there. . . ."

I tuned out her chatter for a minute to process what had just happened: She thought living at Lay to Rest was cool.

I started listening to Johanna again. She was saying ". . . don't tell Nick Wesley, because his dad is the sheriff, but sometimes we go there at night and sneak around in the dark."

That gave me a thought. "You do?"

"Yeah. Oh, please don't tell on us. I shouldn't have said anything."

"No. I won't tell," I promised.

We walked through a big room with long tables. Half of them were low with little preschool-size chairs. Johanna explained, "This is the lunch room.

I have the same thing every day. Chicken spread on an English muffin."

"Yum," I said. I hoped the menu had more variety. I wanted to ask her more about her little cemetery sneaking. "Johanna, did you happen to go to the cemetery last night? Or do you know if someone did?"

"No. Not last night. Yesterday I studied, hung out with Mel at the Pizza Palace—it was her ninth slice, so she got it free. Then I read and went to bed at nine. We would never sneak to the cemetery on a school night."

"Oh." I'd hoped I could explain last night's thuds.

She asked, "Why? Did something happen there last night? I always thought that place was haunted. I mean with all of those dead people, I'd be shocked if it wasn't. I think people know it's haunted, but they're keeping it a secret. I'd love to have a spiritual-aphony and find out. You know, I could totally learn how to do that."

"A spiritual-aphony?" I asked.

"You know, the kind when you summon the dead and talk to them."

"Do you mean a séance?" I asked.

"Yeah. That's what I meant, a séance, but I couldn't think of that word, so I quickly thought up spiritual-aphony. You know, like to call a spirit on the phone?" She put a finger phone—her thumb and pinkie—to her ear.

I nodded, because I got it.

She said, "Have you ever been to a séance? Do they have séances in California?"

"I've never been to one, but I'm sure they exist. I mean, we have *everything* in California. I can't think of anything we don't have: movie stars, surfing, sushi . . ."

"Snow!" Johanna interrupted. "They don't have beautiful, fluffy, white snow, or snowball fights, or snow forts."

"That's true," I said. This girl really didn't care about California. How was that possible?

I heard basketballs bouncing off the walls. "We have gym now." I stood by the door and saw eighth graders bouncing balls and dunking them into baskets that hung so low that they didn't have to jump. A group of boys on scooters were trying to run over each other's fingers. There was no gym teacher to be seen.

"This is gym class?" I asked.

"Actually, it's more like free time," Johanna said.

I followed Johanna into the gym. She stopped at a water fountain and bent very low, Dumb-O height.

I scanned the room for the popular crowd but

couldn't find them. Everyone looked the same: all jeans, T-shirts, many in baseball or snow hats, both boys and girls. Again, I was relieved I'd gone with jeans and a long-sleeved Brandy Melville shirt, which I very subtly untucked more like everyone else's.

A girl with her baseball hat on backward and a 5K FOR KARLEIGH T-shirt walked over, dribbling. "Who are you?" She continued to dribble while checking me out.

I flashed a smile. "Hi, I'm G—"

"G? What kind of a name is that?"

"Oh, no, sorry. It's Sydney. Sydney Mackenzie."

Johanna introduced the girl. "This is Melanie Healey."

"Mel," she corrected. Her face was flat, unfriendly. Mel was taller than me, her legs long and thin. She had hair that looked like it had never seen sun. It was shoulder length with a choppy cut. The only makeup she had on was some black eyeliner. She examined me carefully, but I couldn't tell from her expression if she liked what she saw. "Welcome to the most exciting place on earth." I could tell she meant exactly the opposite.

Johanna said, "You aren't going to believe where she lives, Mel." She didn't give Mel a chance to answer. "At Lay to Rest. The big Victorian. The one in the cemetery at the top of the hill." As though there were more than one.

Johanna's announcement got the attention of the scooter boys. I swallowed and hoped very hard that they, too, would think this was great.

"Really?" Mel asked without indicating if she meant *Really? That's cool,* or *Really? That's yuck.*

Johanna introduced the curly-haired, heavyset boy as Travis. He said, "Hey hey, Cemetery Girl!" and he offered me a high five, which I smacked lightly. "All right," he said, so I guessed I'd slapped okay. He wrapped his arm around a taller, leaner boy. "This here is Nick. He's my best bud." Under his breath he offered me, "The girls think he's cute. I mean look at him. *I* think he's cute." Travis winked at Nick, who shrugged him off, tripped him onto the floor, and held him down with his foot.

"He's an idiot," Nick, who truly was very cute, said. I smiled at how they messed with each other. "Did you just move in?" he asked.

"Yes," I said.

From the ground Travis said, "It must be scary living at Lay to Rest. I heard it's haunted."

Nick pushed his foot harder on Travis's stomach.

"Urgh," Travis moaned.

"Seriously, ignore him," Nick said.

Mel continued dribbling. I still couldn't tell what she thought about me or the cemetery thing, and something told me that her opinion mattered most. "You live in a creepy cemetery," she finally said.

I didn't know what to say, so I just kind of shrugged and looked to Johanna again for a little help. But Johanna and everyone else stared at Mel too.

I held my breath and crossed my fingers.

"That's cool," Mel said. "I've always wanted to go inside that spooky old house."

Phew! "Sure, any time," I replied.

A voice called from the door. "Here she is," Dr. Perkel said to Roz. "You're all set, Miss Mackenzie."

That was my cue to leave. "I guess I'll see you all tomorrow."

Travis started singing the song from *Annie*, "Tomorrow, you're always a day away . . ." Everyone laughed at Jokey Magoo.

Nick rolled his eyes, elbowed Travis in the gut, and said, "See ya."

Johanna waved and smiled big.

Mel tossed a basketball into the low basket. "See ya, Mac," she said.

Mac? Maybe she'd forgotten my real name, but it had a nice ring to it. I had a nickname—definitely a good sign.

Then Mel added, "At the cemetery. See you at the cemetery."

This changed everything.

chapter seven

THE ARMY-NAVY STORE

I WAS STILL TRYING TO GET MY HEAD AROUND the bizarre twist of events that had just happened at the elementary/middle school. I hadn't even given the spooky, creepy old graveyard a chance, and now it seemed like my ticket to Gigi-ism.

I mentally revised the S5:

1. ~~HAVE AN AWESOME LOOK: CLOTHES, HAIR, ETC. . . .~~ BLEND IN.

2. ~~MOST IMPORTANT: DON'T LET ANYONE KNOW ABOUT THE CEMETERY THING~~ LET EVERYONE KNOW THAT I WAS THE ONE WHO LIVED AT THE STATE'S MOST AMAZING CEMETERY.

"Roz, we need to go shopping."

"Forget it. Sydney, I told you—we're on a spending freeze. I don't like it any more than you do. Have you seen my roots?"

I pushed the heat button in the car and shivered. "Not *shopping* shopping, I need some warmer stuff. I'm going to get sick." I sniffled. "Do I have to be cold until May?"

I only had two or three days' worth of Buttermilk River Cove acceptable outfits in my California wardrobe. "Do you want me to get pleurisy, eczema, lupus?"

That got her. Roz pulled up at the army-navy store, which was, as Joyce had indicated, "at the bottom of the hill" from Lay to Rest, along with everything else in the town. "I guess you shouldn't have to freeze until spring."

I had never heard of an army-navy store, but I imagined it was like your average mall store, perhaps military themed, lots of green, tan, and camouflage.

I was wrong.

The store was *actual stuff* that was left over from the army and the navy. I heard Roz say under her breath, "Oh my."

"Oh my" didn't quite capture what we saw.

It was soldier clothes, plus hunting and outdoor stuff.

If Leigh were here, I'd have to call 911, because she'd have a fashion seizure.

We focused on the outdoors section, picking out two turtlenecks, a sweater, a long-sleeved thermal shirt, wool socks, a scarf, and a hat—all khaki. And a Buttermilk Bulldogs sweatshirt.

When we pulled up at home, Jim and Cork were on the roof of the Victorian, hammering. I don't think I'd ever seen Jim with a hammer, or any tool. Cork had no jacket and no shirt under his overalls. He pounded nails with the might of a superhuman. Jim wiped his nose on his jacket sleeve and gave me a really happy face and a wave. Lifting one hand off the roof made him lose his balance.

I watched in horror as he tried to regain his footing, but he was heading toward the edge of the roof.

Cork grabbed the neck of his jacket to pull him back to safety.

Phew.

"Whoa," Jim said. "Thanks a lot."

Cork didn't answer.

"Hold on tighter," I yelled up. "Or you'll be the next customer at Lay to Rest."

"Righto, Syd."

chapter eight

NO BUSINESS LIKE CEMETERY BUSINESS

"COME ON," ELLIOTT SAID. "I'M SUPPOSED to show you the grounds."

I followed him to the workroom, where he tossed his cloak over his shoulders. He flipped the switch to turn off the light, but instead it turned on the outside lights. "Hmm. This hasn't happened in a while."

"What's that?"

"Uhhh, electrical snafus."

"Oh. Maybe I should tell you something," I said. "My dad is working on house projects. And, well, he isn't very good at house projects."

"I don't doubt that, but this ain't him, because he hasn't messed with the lights."

"Then why are they snafued?"

Elliott struggled. "It happens sometimes in these kinds of places."

I wasn't sure if he meant workrooms or houses in general.

He flipped inside and outside switches until he had all the lights turned off. "They usually fix themselves . . . eventually."

Then he looked at me with my arms folded across my midsection. "Are you gonna be warm enough?"

I said, "I don't think I'll be warm enough until July." And I put on my new hat and scarf.

"Well, all the dead make it extra cold here at Lay to Rest."

I stared at him in disbelief. In *Fangs for You* spirits sucked the warmth out of the air. Maybe I could ask Elliott about the thuds.

"I'm *kidding*," Elliott said. "Geez. I got you with that one."

I let out a weak laugh, because I didn't think it was funny, and followed him out the back. When he wasn't looking, I exhaled and examined the white puff of my breath.

Elliott stopped and opened his arms wide. "Welcome to the graveyard. My job is to keep the grounds maintained. But I go one step further and really make them snappy. Do you see how I trimmed the evergreens over there so that people can walk the path without worrying the boughs will hit them on the head?"

Whose job is it to manage the ghosts? "Uh-huh."

"I took those trimmed branches and pruned them into nice little sprigs, which I tied together with a light wire. See the swags of green garland draped from the mausoleum roofs? It adds a little color."

Elliott was the Martha Stewart of cemeteries. "Exactly what is a mausoleum? I mean, what's inside those buildings?" Cemetery knowledge was going to be important to my rise in popularity.

"They're buildings in which people can be encased instead of being buried." He weaved among a row of structures, and I followed. "Families own these to house several ancestors in one place."

"Oh." *Majorly creepy Magoo.*

"There are sixty rows of graves. Each row is fifty graves long and two deep. That's how we refer to their locations. For example this is row twelve, grave number ten. The bottom grave is called B, the top is A. So this plot is 12-10A."

"What do you mean 'two deep'?"

"That means that a couple, like a married couple, can buy one grave plot, but both corpses can be buried in it, one on top of another, for all eternity."

I shivered. It seemed Elliott liked talking about corpses and dead bodies. Maybe he could tell I was getting uncomfortable, because he explained the rest more basically. "One is buried seven feet deep, and the other three and a half feet deep. It saves space and it saves people money."

"How many *people*"—I didn't know what word to use—"are buried here?"

"We have about twenty-five hundred souls on our property, and room for at least three thousand more. There's plenty of room for many years to come. Your parents have made a good investment. I wish I could've bought her myself."

Part of me wished he *had* bought her and I could be back in California. Another part of me was glad he hadn't, because Lay to Rest was giving me a chance to be the Gigi. A chance I wouldn't have had in California. "And how old is this place?"

"Many of the original records have been lost, but the oldest headstone she has is from 1602. You know, lots of history here. I sometimes wonder about all the stories this place could tell. That's over a hundred and seventy years before the Declaration of Independence was signed." He smiled proudly.

"Wow." It was pretty amazing.

From where Elliott and I now stood at the top of the hill, I could see into the entire cove. Little houses and streets were plotted among a layer of gray slush. It seemed like the most insignificant place in the world, but not to Elliott, and not to Roz and Jim and Uncle Ted and Johanna. And, I guess, not to me.

There was one house that stood out because it was bigger and farther away from everything else. "Who lives there?" I asked.

"Mrs. Dolan. Let's just say she doesn't go out much."

"Why?"

"She's not popular around these parts," he said.

"How come?"

"People think her family is cursed."

My throat dropped into my chest, and my belly flipped. "Cursed?"

"Her ancestors were witches, they say."

For a second I thought I'd have to live in a town without a curse of a witch. *Phew.*

The witch-curse thing didn't faze Elliott because he just continued bragging about the town. "Buttermilk

River Cove is a great place. Some people say John Hancock may have stopped here on his way to sign the Declaration of Independence."

"Neat."

He reached under his cloak into a pocket and pulled out a rag with which he wiped bird poop off a tombstone. "We get a lot of birds on account of the birdhouses and feeders I've nailed along that row of tall oaks. Do you see them?"

I couldn't miss them; they'd been painted bright red.

"I think people like to see birds flying when they visit. Their chirping is comforting to them, I think."

"I like birds." I knew it sounded stupid, but I didn't have anything else nice to offer. John Hancock was boring, it was cold, and I was still preoccupied by the cursed witch.

Our expedition complete, Elliott surveyed the whole property we'd just walked. "Yup," he said. "She is really special."

"She does seem special," I agreed. I just had to start believing it. The wind blew and a twig snapped underfoot, making me jump.

"You okay?" he asked.

"Fine." Before I could like Lay to Rest I'd have to

get past the fact that it scared the bejesus out of me.

"You'll get used to it," he said, seeming to know what I was thinking. "Give it some time."

He held the back door open for me, and after four tries he found the light switch that worked.

"What's in there?" I asked about a door.

"That goes down to the cold room. That's where bodies used to be stored before burials. Your dad has big plans to transform that room." At that, the lights went out. "Oh, stop that," he said to no one in particular, and he flipped the switch back on.

"What was that?"

"Like I said, that happens sometimes, but I have to admit, it's never been this bad." Then he said, "Let's see if Joyce can get us some hot cocoa."

"Now you're speaking my language," I said.

Joyce stood in the kitchen–meeting room, which was dark despite several candles. She stirred a tall wooden spoon in circles inside a big black pot. The steam wrapped around her like ribbons of dense fog. "Cocoa?"

"Yes, please," I said.

"And how about a toasted muffin?"

"That sounds great."

Joyce sliced a muffin in half and spread creamy

white butter on either half and plopped them, butter side down, on a griddle. I expected a sizzle, but the griddle wasn't hot.

She laughed awkwardly and sent an eye message to Elliott.

"I know," he said. "It just started yesterday."

She eyed him again, sending another message.

"It will go away. Don't worry—"

"Don't worry about what?" I asked. "That Jim isn't handy? I've known that for a long time."

She smiled, looking at Elliott, not me. Then she asked him, "Be a dear and hand me those mugs."

She ladled the hot liquid into the mugs. "Here we go. Two cocoas, hold the eye of newt."

I laughed awkwardly. She was kidding, obviously. *Right?*

I sipped cautiously. "Yum."

"It's made with buttermilk," she said with a wink. "That's my secret."

"I won't tell anyone," I said.

"It's okay. Nothing is a secret around here. It's a small town . . . everybody knows everything."

When it was ready, I bit into a toasty, crispy, buttery corn muffin. It was fantastic.

"What does your father have planned for the

basement?" Joyce asked. A breeze flew through the kitchen, causing the candle flames to quiver.

"I heard him say a yoga or game room."

Elliott said, "It will need a lot of demo work before renovations can begin."

The dim kitchen light began to blink—on, off, on, off.

"Just a snafu with the wiring," Elliott said.

Joyce said, "We both know it has nothing to do with wiring."

chapter nine

VISITORS

I DIDN'T GET TO ASK WHAT JOYCE MEANT about the wiring because we interrupted by a knock.

I moved through the Victorian to the front door. I opened it to see a large, plump man with sideburns the shape of Texas.

"Well, hello there. You must be Sydney," he said with a deep, low voice. "I'm Mr. Margreither."

I recognized the name from hearing my parents talk about him. He was the mayor of Buttermilk River Cove. "Hello, Mayor Margreither."

"I just stopped by to introduce myself in the flesh and blood. No more phone and e-mail. Are your folks here?"

I heard the vacuum running, telling me Roz was upstairs, and I heard hammering, which probably meant Jim was working on the roof again. I hoped he didn't hammer himself to the shingles. "Sure. Come in."

Joyce walked up behind me. "Why hello, Mayor Margreither. I'm sure you're looking for the Mackenzies. I'll get them for you."

"Thank you, Joyce. It's a pleasure to see you." Then Mayor Margreither asked me, "How are you finding Buttermilk River Cove?"

"So far, so good."

"Have you made any friends?"

"My first day of school isn't officially until tomorrow, but I went in today and met a bunch of the kids," I said.

Two figures walked up the sidewalk toward the house. "Speak of the devil," he said. "Here comes the queen of Buttermilk River Cove Middle School herself."

I wanted to correct him and explain that it was an elementary *and* middle school in one building designed for extras from the *Wizard of Oz*'s Munchkinland, but I didn't. Melanie Healey and a woman I assumed was her mother came up the driveway. "Oh, Mayor Margreither! What a lovely surprise to see you here!" Mrs. Healey exclaimed.

Mayor Margreither said, "Hello, Jennifer. Hello, Melanie."

Joyce returned with Roz and Jim, then left to make coffee. Mrs. Healey handed Roz a package in which she said there was a fresh duck, a gift to welcome us to Buttermilk River Cove. I wasn't certain, but I thought I saw a webbed foot sticking out of the bag. *Ew.*

Roz thanked Mrs. Healey holding the bag as far away from her as possible, then said to me, "Why don't you show your friend around? You're Melanie, right?"

"Mel," Mel corrected Roz.

"Sure," I said. "Come on, Mel."

I figured that making a good impression was very important. I showed her the percolator and griddle, then the office, which I'd not been in yet.

Melanie let out a loud sigh. I was boring her.

Then we entered a big room with a fireplace. The windows on each side were covered by long, heavy, dark drapes.

Melanie asked. "Is this where you keep the coffins?"

"I don't know," I said. Mel's eyes glossed over.

I thought. "Um, I think this is known as the Last Chance Room. It's the last time people get to see someone's body before it goes into the ground." I carefully watched her expression. "Deep, deep into the earth in a locked box forever . . . and ever."

"Yeah?" She wanted to hear more.

"Actually, this room got its name when John Hancock—you know he was one of the signers of the Declaration of Independence?—well, he had died and he was supposed to be buried here. His wife came in and lifted the lid of his casket to give him one last kiss before he was buried for all eternity. And when she touched his lips, he moved."

"He did?"

I was on a roll. "Yeah."

"And then what happened?"

I thought of a scene from *White Beach*. "He kissed her back—a big passionate kiss. Then he sat up and wrapped his arms around her. I think she climbed in the coffin with him and they kissed for, like, a really long time." (The part about the coffin wasn't from *White Beach*.)

She nodded. "Wow, cool."

"Yeah, totally cool. So you see if he didn't get that last chance, we might still be a colony of England, right?"

She hung on every word.

"This room is super important to American history."

Mel's eyes begged for more details, which I offered.

"From then on all the dead bodies hang out in this room for a certain amount of time, like a day or eight hours, before being buried, just to make sure that the person isn't going to come back to life." Mel was totally buying it. Maybe we could get froyo together one day. If Buttermilk River Cove had froyo, that is.

Mel said, "That's a good story, Mac. I hadn't heard that one before, and I thought I knew everything about Buttermilk River Cove."

I smiled at her.

I was going to make this the coolest cemetery ever.

chapter ten

THE FIRST DAY OF SCHOOL

WHETHER YOU LIVED IN CALIFORNIA OR Delaware, the real test of popularity was in the same place—the school cafeteria. I was nervous to enter the caf the first day of school. I really wished Leigh were here.

I remembered my movie preview where everybody wanted me to sit at their table. Today I just hoped one person, preferably a non-booger-eater, would invite me to sit with them.

I saw One and Two right away. They were sitting with a bunch of other first graders. They chugged chocolate milk out of little boxes and burped the "Star-Spangled Banner." They were the hit of the table. The Dumb-Os were "in" already.

I wandered around the caf checking to see if I got

any strange looks at my new turtleneck, new scarf, or old boot-cut jeans. I didn't. Although, maybe my black leather boots with an itty-bitty heel got some double takes.

When I saw Mel and Johanna, they waved me over to sit with them.

YES!

"Hey," I said.

Mel was drawing on her sneakers with a permanent marker, the cap in her teeth. "Hey, Cemetery Girl. I had the heebie-jeebies all night after I left your house."

I hesitantly eased into a seat. *Heebie-jeebies are bad, right?* Had something changed and cemeteries weren't cool anymore? "You did?"

"Yeah," she said. "I love spooky stuff. Don't you?"

Phew!

"Welcome to my life. All spooky, all the time," I said. "I love it too."

Mel said, "I told everyone about the Last Chance Room and that story. They want to see it."

"Really? I mean, sure, that would be great. Any time. My crypt door is always open."

They laughed. (Maybe I was good at cemetery humor.)

My stomach growled. Maybe some sushi or grilled Swiss with sun-dried tomato on rye would hit the spot. I asked, "Where's the line?"

"The milk line?" Mel indicated a row of short kids. "It's over there."

"What about the food?" I asked.

Mel and Johanna looked at me like I was a zombie. "We bring our own lunch," Johanna said. "This isn't like a lunch-au-rant."

Mel looked at me. "She means restaurant."

"How about a salad bar?" I asked.

They shook their heads, confused.

"Frozen yogurt machine?"

Mel asked, "You're kidding, right?"

I shrugged. Mel tossed me a skinny pepperoni thing. I'd heard of Slim Jims but never actually had one. I tore the plastic and apprehensively took a bite. It was greasy and spicy and totally yummy. Leigh would die if she saw me eating a stick of processed meat.

"Thanks," I said, and before I knew it, I also had half of a chicken spread on English muffin sandwich and a fistful of Crunch 'n Munch from Johanna.

Johanna asked, "Does your house have a bell tower? I always thought that a hunchback who ate bugs lived in the attic. I think it was from some ghost story that my cousin told me one time. She told me that story and another one about the Dolans being cursed."

Mel said, "Everybody knows that one."

I rounded my back. "Nah. No hunchbacks, just me."

They all laughed again. I was a hit! Somehow in the backward land of Buttermilk River Cove, Delaware, the girl who lived at the cemetery in an old Victorian house with weird graveyard workers was *in!*

Mel went back to drawing on her shoes. "So what do you do for fun, Mac?" she asked.

"I like the beach in California. My friends and I spend a lot of time at the beach swimming, getting tans, even surfing."

I expected them to say, *The Beach!, Surfing!, That's so cool!, Tell us about it!* Instead, Mel said, "You won't find big waves here."

Then I said, "I used to be in school plays."

Johanna asked, "You're an actress? That sounds like fun, huh, Mel?" Mel shrugged a little. "What kind of plays?"

"I was supposed to be in *Romeo and Juliet* before I moved. It's my dream to be in a movie someday. When is your next school play? I'd like to audition."

Mel snorted.

"What?" I asked in response to the snort. "You don't think I can get a part in the next school play?"

"Oh, I think you could get the lead," she spit out with a laugh.

"Oh, thanks." I didn't know what was funny.

Johanna covered up her amusement. "She thinks it's funny that you think we have a school play."

"You don't?"

Johanna shook her head.

"What about the drama department?" I asked. "Improv class?"

Johanna shook her head again.

Mel added, "We don't have squat around here."

Johanna corrected her, "We have a hockey team. They won the Delaware State Championships in 1974."

No school play? "Hockey's good. What else do you guys do around here?"

They looked at one another and kind of shrugged. "We hang out at the Pizza Palace," Mel said.

Johanna added, "They have a club card. You get the ninth slice free."

"Great," I said. I added it up. They have hockey and pizza. I might have some free time on my hands.

Then Johanna said, "Sometimes Nick's dad clears

the snow off the lake and we ice skate. And in the summer we do bonfires at the lake."

"That sounds like fun. I've never been ice-skating," I said. "Do you like the movies?"

Johanna said, "There's a theater in Wilmington. It's too far to walk. Mel's mom took us to see *Fangs for You*. Have you seen it?"

"Yeah, like five times."

"Five times?" Mel said, "I guess you love it."

"Makes sense that you'd like scary movies," Johanna said. "Being in the cemetery business an' all."

I nodded. You'd expect someone to love a movie they'd seen five times, except that *Fangs* scared the crap out of me, and I only saw it five times because it was all the rage and Leigh wanted to.

The table fell silent as the conversation started to die an awkward death.

"You guys have to come over and get a full tour of the graveyard," I finally said. "Mel only saw some of the inside. There's way more creepy stuff."

Johanna's eyes lit up. "Like what?"

I said, "Like mausoleums."

"Are those like crypts?" Mel asked.

"I guess so," I said. I made a mental note to google crypts and mausoleums.

"I'm free today," Johanna said.

Mel said, "Today's good."

I said, "Then today it is."

Just then Travis bumped into the table and helped himself to a seat. "What's today?" He picked up Mel's other Slim Jim, bit it, and put it back.

Johanna said, "We're going to Mac's to check out the crypts."

He said, "I'm in."

Nick came up behind Travis and said, "In what?"

"A little crypty fiesta at Casa Creepy," Travis said.

"What the heck does that mean?" Nick asked.

Mel translated. "We're going over Mac's after school."

"Over *Mac's*?" he asked me with raised eyebrows, as if to say, You *have a nickname?* I *don't have a nickname.*

I nodded. "You wanna come?"

"Sounds like a plan." Nick held up his fist. I bumped it.

Thank goodness I live in a cemetery.

chapter eleven

MAUSOLEUMS

AFTER SCHOOL I WALKED UP THE HILL toward the Victorian. Johanna, Mel, Travis, and Nick were coming over after they dropped their school stuff off at home. I ran to my computer to check e-mail. I got one from Leigh . . . Yay!

> *Hey Syd,*
>
> *Sorry it took me a few days to write back. It's just that I text everyone. Did you get a new phone yet?*
>
> *I saw the preview for* Terror on the Train *starring Dylan Posencheg. I can't wait to see it. Oh, and I got that Guess bikini we saw a few weeks ago. Anyway, write me back and tell me about life with the dead. . . .*

I guess that's better than life with the undead. Hahaha! LOL

> *<3, Leigh*

I wrote back.

> *Hi Leigh,*
>
> *Something strange has happened here: The kids don't think California stuff is cool. Crazy, right? Did I mention the house we live in is actually ON the cemetery? Like IN it! What's even crazier is that the kids think the cemetery is awesome. Actually, 4 new friends are coming over today. So I'm going to act like I think it's as exciting as they do.*
>
> *Oh, and it might be haunted.*
>
> *Ta, Dahling. ☺ Syd.*

When the girls arrived, I gave the standard disclaimer. "I have two little brothers. They're six. They're twins. They're annoying."

"Okay," Johanna said, but I could tell she didn't know what I was talking about. Not many people *really* understood what it was like to have twin brothers. They *thought* they understood because maybe they had a younger brother or sister. Maybe they thought you multiplied the annoyance times two. But really it was multiplied by like five hundred.

I added, "It's possible they were dropped on their heads as babies. I just want you to know up front that I don't think I'm actually related to them." This got a smirk of approval from Mel.

Travis and Nick arrived a few minutes later.

Travis examined every nook and cranny of the foyer as he walked into the Victorian. "Wow. I've always wanted to see inside this place." He studied and squinted at a strange section of wall, then he knocked on it. "Hear that?" He knocked on a different section and then back on the first spot. "It's hollow."

"So?" Johanna asked.

"So . . . there could be passages behind these walls," he said. Then he asked me, "Have you checked it out?"

"Seriously?" I asked. "Like on *Scooby-Doo*?"

Nick said, "It isn't that unusual in big old houses." He was serious.

"Why would they need secret passages?" I asked.

"To hide," Mel said, but she said it like *duh*.

Nick added, "To hide people or things. During

the Civil War people hid their silver and stashes of money. They sometimes hid their teenage boys so that they wouldn't be drafted to the war. Or people hid from the Confederate Army when they came into town." He sounded really smart. "I guess. I'm not actually sure." But I thought he did know, he just didn't want to sound too smart.

I noticed Johanna stretching her neck to see into the workroom.

"You guys want a tour of the spooky old place?" I used my most enthusiastic voice. "Want to see a mausoleum?"

"Heck yeah," Travis said.

They followed me through the house, spending extra time in the Last Chance Room.

Travis asked, "What *is* the difference between a crypt and a mausoleum?"

Johanna answered before I had a chance, "I think one has mummies and is haunted."

"Oh, don't worry, I don't think that's the kind we have," I said.

"Bummer," Nick said.

Whoa! He wants this place to be haunted? What kind of town is this?

Mel said, "Let's find out."

"Let's do it!" I said way more excitedly than I felt.

I led them to the graveyard. It took effort, but I tried to walk normally among the tombstones, as if stepping on dead bodies didn't bother me at all. Mel and Johanna followed my lead. They seemed to have no problem walking on the dead. In my head I still whispered, "Sorry, sorry, sooo sorry."

I explained the rows and the buried two-deep thing to them the way I would explain a new froyo flavor to Leigh. *There are delicious swirls of raspberry and an incredible hint of coconut flavor that you're gonna love. I got two cherries and these amazing cookie crunches on top.* Instead what I said was something like, "One corpse is placed in a deep dark hole, about seven feet down, and covered with dirt. It might be down there for a long time, rotting, until the owner of the second spot dies. The ground is dug up again, but not as deep this time because you don't want to disturb a rotting corpse."

"Why not?" Travis asked.

"Umm. I think it's bad luck," I said like I was some kind of expert.

We approached a mausoleum. An eerie wind blew clouds in front of the sun, creating a bleakness that was typical of Buttermilk River Cove.

[Some low and frightening music plays—like a deep churchy pipe organ.]

Mel put a hand out to touch the stones. Johanna and I did the same. They were cold and damp. Cemented to the stones was a small plaque with the names of the people inside. HANNAH DOLAN: DEVOTED MOTHER AND AUNT. HAYDEN DOLAN: LOVING WIFE. This looked like it belonged to the Dolan family, because most of the last names were Dolan, except for one. I figured they were all related somehow. I had cousins whose last names weren't Mackenzie.

"The Dolans are cursed," Johanna said.

"That's about the most exciting thing we've got around here," Mel said.

Travis added, "And our hockey team kicks butt."

I asked, "Wasn't that like forty-something years ago?"

Mel looked at me like it was *not* okay that I suggested the hockey team's winning streak was old news. "They're still really good."

I nodded. Message received: It was okay for Mel to say Buttermilk River Cove was boring but not for me.

I looked up and noticed small marble cherubs (baby angels) carved into the roof. Mel stood on her tiptoes to reach one but couldn't. She reached for the door handle and pushed, but it didn't open. She turned the handle again and shoved a hip into the door. It budged. She pushed with her whole side. I helped with both hands. The two of us slowly slid the heavy door. It made a terrible scratching against the cement floor.

A dust blob flew out of the pitch black and landed on my face. *Gross!*

Johanna was behind me. "Go on," she nudged.

Hair on the back of my neck stood up. "Wait," I said.

"What?" Mel asked, clearly annoyed.

I needed to stall or change their minds. "Where are the boys?" Suddenly going into a cursed family's mausoleum felt like a bad idea.

Mel said, "Who cares?" She pressed forward and stepped over the threshold. "Probably chickened out."

I took a deep breath of musty air and entered too.

"I can't see a thing," Johanna said. I heard her take a baby step closer to me.

My heart raced. I begged my eyes to adjust to the darkness, but they didn't.

I just stood still.

Then all of the sudden a voice behind me screamed: "BOOOO!"

Another went: "Moooohahahahhha!

We all screamed!

Mel backed into me. She stepped on my foot, and I bit my tongue.

My heart stopped beating for just a second. I ran outside, pushing Johanna in front of me. Mel was on my heels.

Travis and Nick rolled on the cold, damp grass, laughing.

I caught my breath. The three of us stood over them. Johanna and I had our hands on our hips; Mel's arms were crossed in front of her chest.

The boys didn't stop their hooting and laughing.

Mel kicked Travis (not too hard) right in the butt, leaving a muck mark.

"You jerkazoids!" Johanna yelled.

"You should've seen your faces," Travis said, almost crying-laughing. "You were like, *Ahhhh!* I thought your hair would stand straight up on end. I wish I had a camera."

Once I was breathing normally, I cracked a half smile. They had gotten us good. And they looked so funny, rolling around laughing on the ground.

"Mooohahahaa," Nick said to Travis in between laughs, and that started them all over again.

"Dude," Travis said. "Stop it. You're gonna make me pee myself."

Johanna said, "You guys are real morons, you know that?"

Mel ignored them, like they were totally immature. She turned back to the small building to continue her tour.

Just then Cork came from behind the mausoleum. "Hey! What are you kids doing?" he grouched.

"I was just showing them around," I explained.

He pulled the mausoleum door shut, tight. "You shouldn't be messing in other people's private places."

Mel harrumphed.

"Fine," I said, as though I was equally disappointed, but inside I wanted to jump up and kiss that man. (Okay, maybe I didn't want to actually *kiss* him, but I was glad he came when he did.)

The boys got off the ground and wiped the dirt from their clothes.

We walked together back toward the Victorian. Mel said, "That guy is totally creepy."

"Yup," I agreed.

"He looks like Godzilla with that zipper scar on his head," Johanna said.

"I think you mean Frankenstein," Travis corrected.

"Godzilla is a giant lizard that terrorizes Tokyo. Frankenstein is the one that was sewn together from parts of different people."

Elliott got to the back door just when we did. His cloak was tied around his neck. His arms were full of green holly branches.

As we went inside, I introduced Elliott to my friends, and when he dropped the greens on the table, he reached for their hands. *"Enchanté."*

"Your hands are freezing," Johanna complained.

"It's pretty cold out there," he said.

"I love holly. What are you going to do with it?" She touched the prickly leaves.

"I thought I'd decorate the hearth."

Elliott looked at Johanna's hand, which had a few droplets of red on it. "Oh my, is that blood?" He whipped his head in the opposite direction. "I can't stand the sight of blood."

"It's okay," Johanna said. "Really, it's nothing."

"I hate blood." He still didn't look at her.

Johanna put her hand out. "Seriously, it's just juice from one of the holly berries."

Elliott turned with an embarrassed laugh. He scooped up his branches and left the workroom. We went into the kitchen and sat down.

"I don't think I've ever seen anyone so scared of the sight of blood," I said.

Nick said, "You're around scary stuff all the time, so it's no big whoop to you. You're used to it."

"I guess." If he only knew the truth.

"Or," Johanna said, "maybe he's a vampire."

Travis asked, "JoJo, you know vampires are *make-believe*?" He said "make-believe" slowly so she would understand.

"What are you talking about?" she asked. "Didn't you see *Fangs for You*?"

"That's a movie. It's pretend," Travis said.

Nick whispered to Travis, "She's kidding you." Although I didn't think she was, and I think Nick knew that; he just wanted Travis to leave her alone. Then Nick said, "Besides, vampires aren't afraid of blood—they love it."

"But maybe," I said to help Johanna out, "he's a vampire who wants to live with mortals, so he controls his lust for human blood, but if he sees it, he won't be able to, and he'll jump on you and suck you dry." That would make a good movie plot.

"I know I'd like to suck some hot cocoa," Travis said. "And I smell some."

I walked over to the pot on the stove and stirred

it just to make sure Joyce hadn't added any newt eyes (or any other kind of eyes or ears) when no one was around. It looked good. Actually, it looked great. I ladled out five small mugs. We sat at the table talking, me and my four new friends. They thought the cocoa was awesome. I explained it was made with buttermilk. It felt good to have everyone hanging out with me.

That's when it happened:

One and Two.

They came into the kitchen.

Nothing good was going to come of this.

chapter twelve

POP. POP. POP.

ONE GRABBED A COOKIE IN EACH HAND.

Two kicked Nick in the shins.

"Ouch. What was that for?"

Two said, "Just 'cause your friends with poop-head Sydney."

One said, "You know, she used to pretend she was rich and fancy in California just to be popular."

Heat engulfed my face. "What? I didn't pretend."

"She seems pretty fancy to me," Travis said.

"She wouldn't need to pretend," Nick added.

The twins started jumping up and down on one foot. Not for any reason. "Well, she did. She pretended lots of stuff, like she had a credit card when she didn't," One said.

Two added, "Just to fit in."

"Pop. Pop. Pop," they sang while they jumped.

"Don't listen to them," I said. "I told you, annoying."

"Pop. Pop. Pop."

"Fitting in is important to some people," Nick said.

"Oooh," One said, still jumping. "You like Sydney."

Two asked him, "What's your name?"

"Nick.

"Nick likes Sydney! Nick likes Sydney!" they sang.

If there was any minute to climb into a mausoleum and curl into a ball and die, this was it. Mel said to them, "Why don't you hop out of here before I pop you right in the mouth?"

They stopped hopping and stared at her, stupefied. They slowly inched toward the door. Then, just before leaving, One snatched cookies and Two bent down, stuck out his butt, and made farting sounds with his lips. He toppled over, hitting his head on the floor. "Awww!" he yelled, and rubbed his head. "Why'd you do that?" Two asked One.

"Do what?"

"Push me."

One said, "I didn't."

"Did too."

"Did not." Then One stuck his butt toward Two

and made a fart noise with *his* lips and ran out of the kitchen.

Two chased after him.

The room was silent after that.

"I'm so sorry," I said. "I warned you."

"You understated how annoying they were," Johanna said.

Then Mel asked, "Did you really pretend to have a credit card?"

chapter thirteen

HORROR FILM

THAT NIGHT I CALLED LEIGH. AS THE PHONE rang, I thought about how stupid the twins had made me feel with the credit card comment. Luckily, I was able to explain that they were just Dumb-Os.

"Chell-o, Syd," Leigh answered. "How goes it out east?"

"All spooky, all the time," I said.

"Really. Still?"

"Actually, I'm starting to get used to it." I had no reason to pretend anything with Leigh anymore. "My new friends really like the cemetery."

"Ugh. Then you need to find some new friends."

"I don't think so. I like them."

"Then," Leigh said, "I guess it's a good thing you have a cemetery."

"Yeah." I laughed a little. "The only thing that would make it better, make me the real Gigi, would be if it was haunted. They'd love that."

"So, do it."

"What?" I asked.

"Syd, if they want a haunted cemetery, then give them one. You wanna be the Gigi of Spookytown, so get on it, Magoo. You're an actress—act like it's haunted." She added, "Oh, gotta run." And the line went dead.

I might not have to *act*. . . .

I thought about what it could be like if Lay to Rest was haunted.

Scene:

> *My new friends and I are playing Monopoly on the kitchen table when there's a clattering and a howl from outside.*
>
> *"What's that?" Johanna asks.*
>
> *"Oh, what? That noise?" I ask, like it's no biggie. "That's just the ghost of Gavin Poole." I point to the clock. "He always howls around seven." I go to the window and yell out, "Keep it down, Gavin! We're playing a game, and I own Boardwalk and Park Place!"*

They look at me.

"Wow. That was cool," Mel says.

"You're so brave," Travis says.

Nick doesn't say anything at first. He just stares at me. I realize how deep dark blue his eyes are. When the other three huddle around the window hoping for a glimpse of Gavin, Nick says, "Maybe you want to go to Pizza Palace tomorrow after school. Just us?"

My mental movie clip was interrupted with *thud!* There it was again.

[A few bars of spooky music.]

Big branches brushed against my window and I heard *snap—crack—snap.* It sounded like someone, or something, walking on the frozen cemetery ground outside. Or was the sound coming from outside my door? It was hard to tell with the wind.

Bravely I crept to the window and opened the slits of the mini blinds just enough to see a sliver of the moon. It wasn't giving off much light through the clouds. I squinted and saw a birdhouse sway. It creaked on its hook and thumped against the tree trunk, too softly to be the thud.

Then *thud!*

I dashed down the hall into the Dumb-Os' room. I slipped under the covers of the bottom bunk with One . . . or maybe it was Two. I couldn't tell when they were asleep. Come to think of it, I could hardly tell when they were awake. I was really mad at them, but now I snuggled this twin like he was a security blanket.

I lay there and wondered how awesome my friends would think it was if Lay to Rest was haunted.

* chapter fourteen *
THINGS THAT THUD

I STOPPED IN THE KITCHEN ON MY WAY OUT to school. There were dirty bowls and spoons and eggshells and flour and cinnamon sprinkled all over the place.

One and Two took turns holding the maple syrup bottle upside down, squeezing and drinking from it.

Roz stood at the stove.

"What happened in here?" My first thought was that zombies had left their graves during the night, decided they were hungry, and rummaged through our cabinets. Even the undead have to eat, right?

"I'm making breakfast," Roz said.

"How's that working out?" I asked.

One cracked an egg on his head.

Roz said, "No wonder you have a bruise on your

head, if you're bopping yourself with things like that." Roz wiped her brow with the back of her wrist, leaving a smear of white flour. "I'm not going to lie to you, Syd. The French toast isn't going well."

The percolator angrily spit crud into the clear lid. She saw me checking it out. "The coffee didn't go well either."

"How about some orange juice?" I asked.

She smiled. "I can do that." She handed me the carton and a glass.

Roz looked at the plate of yucky French toast. I didn't think she wanted to give it to the twins.

"You know," I said. "They'll eat anything with syrup on it."

chapter fifteen

THE KING OF SECRETS

I SAT WITH MEL AND JOHANNA AT LUNCH.

Johanna was saying, "But it was my ninth slice. So it was free."

"That's great, but now you have to start all over," Mel said.

"That's okay. After eight slices, I'll get another." Then Johanna said to me, "We stopped at the Palace after leaving your house last night, and I got a free slice. I swear, it tasted better than a regular slice."

"Really?" I asked, but all I thought was why hadn't they invited me? My stomach instantly tied into a knot, and I couldn't drink my carton of school milk. Maybe they didn't like me as much as I thought.

"Maybe we'll do it this weekend," Johanna said about something, but I didn't know what.

"Sure," Mel said.

Were they doing something without me this weekend?

I leaned in closer to the girls. "I have a little problem," I said. "Can you keep a secr—"

Nick and Travis came out of nowhere and sat across from us. "A secret?" Travis asked. "I love secrets. What's the secret?"

Johanna said to Travis, "It only stays a secret if you keep it a secret. And everyone knows you *can't*."

Travis tapped his chest. "Me? I am like the king of secrets. I can keep a secret like nobody's business. Isn't that right, Nick? Can't I keep a secret like nobody's business? Remember how I never told anyone about that time in first grade when you peed in your pants in art class because Mr. Schuldner wouldn't give you a bathroom pass?" He shoved an entire Devil Dog in his mouth.

"Sure," Nick said. "You're the king of secrets. And the duke of Devil Dogs."

Travis smiled with black cake in between his teeth.

I looked at Nick and remembered how he asked me out for pizza in my movie preview.

"What?" he asked when he caught me staring. "Booger?"

I shook my head. "Nothing."

I guess he didn't believe me that it was nothing, because he wiped his nose anyway.

Mel said, "Don't worry about him. If he tells anyone, I'll get Gary and Quincy to paste his underpants over his head."

Johanna whispered to me, "They're her cousins. They lay cement. With that stuff, it would take a while to loosen underwear."

Travis swallowed. "Like I said, I can keep a secret."

Nick leaned in on both elbows, listening. "Me too," he said. I snuck another stare at him.

Mel asked, "So, what's this BIIIIG secret?"

"I was going to tell you yesterday, but I wanted to be sure first. Well, I'm still not *sure* sure, but I'm kinda sure. I'm more sure than yesterday, because it happened again."

"What happened?" Nick asked.

I darted my eyes back and forth, because that's what people in the movies do before they make a big statement like this. They were all listening. "I think Lay to Rest is haunted."

Their eyes popped. Like I'd hoped, they were totally into it. They looked like Leigh when she walked into Saks when it was decorated for Christmas.

I was totally on my way to Gigi-ism.

"You *think*?" Mel asked.

"Well, yeah. Maybe a little," I said.

"Can you have just a *little* haunting?" Johanna asked. "Are there different sizes, like with a fountain soda: small, medium, large, and super-extra jumbo?"

"Um, I don't know. This is all kind of new to me."

Travis asked, "I wonder if there's a test. Like if you think you have mice, you know because you see stuff chewed up. If you have deer eating your corn, you can see their hoofprints. How would you know for sure? It's not like we can leave a note that says, 'Check yes if you're haunting Lay to Rest.' And what if they're haunting you, but they decide to be funny and check no."

Nick asked, "You wanna leave a note for a ghost and ask him to check a box?" His tone said, *Are you serious, moron?*

Travis said, "I was just thinking. You know, like how could we find out? Mac said she isn't sure. She didn't, like, interview the ghosts, or did you? Did you actually talk to any spirits?"

"Umm. No. I . . . um . . . no, I didn't."

"See," Travis said. "She didn't talk to any ghosts. If she had, then we would have our answers. I was just trying to come up with some other ideas. But I can tell by the look on all of your faces that you don't appreciate my ideas." He popped an Oreo into his mouth.

I explained the thuds.

Mel said, "A thud could be a lot of things."

"How can we find out for sure?"

Johanna said, "A spiritual-aphony."

We looked at her strangely.

"We have a séance at the cemetery and see if there is a spirit hanging around," she explained like we were dunces.

I didn't love that idea. "Ummm," I said.

Mel even said, "It's a *great* idea."

"What I mean is, should we disturb the spirit world? We could open some portal we can't close, and Buttermilk River Cove would be overrun with ghosts or zombies," I said. "That's what always happens in the movies."

Well, *that* clearly was the wrong thing to say.

"Zombies!" Travis said. "Seriously? That would be so awesome, dude. Think about it. We'd be on the news."

Mel asked Johanna, "Do you know how to do that? A séance?"

"How hard can it be?" she asked. "I'll look it up. By Friday I'll be a pro."

Mel looked at me; maybe she sensed that I was nervous. "What's the worst thing that could happen?"

I didn't answer, but the worst that could happen was we could find out it wasn't haunted and my quest could be over forever, or we could find out it was haunted and then, well, I'd be haunted!

They agreed: Friday, eight o'clock, behind the Dolan mausoleum.

"How exciting! A séance. I can't wait," I lied.

Johanna ran out of the caf ahead of us to get a book from the library. Travis followed her. Mel picked up her things when the bell rang. I tossed my trash. When I came back to the table, Nick was holding up my backpack by its handle.

"Thanks," I said.

We walked in the same direction to fifth period.

"So, a séance?" he said as we bumped through the crowd like pinballs.

"Sounds like fun, right?" A short kid walked into my stomach, then changed his route.

"Sure. If it works, it should tell you what you're dealing with."

"*If* it works?" I asked.

"Are you thinking Johanna can perform a real séance and communicate with the dead and ask them if they're haunting you?" He stopped at his cubby, Buttermilk River Cove Middle School's excuse for lockers, and swapped out some books. "I don't think she can, and I don't think she can learn by Friday. Do you?"

"I don't know." I considered it. "She seemed pretty confident."

"Well it's not like we have anything else to do around here." He zippered his pack. "What are you doing this afternoon?" he asked, and I thought this was the moment when he'd ask me to the Pizza Palace.

"I have some chores. Why?"

"Just wondering," he said.

"Were you thinking of going to the Pizza Palace?" I asked.

"Not really. I have to work today."

"Oh." I flushed with embarrassment. Of course he wasn't asking me to the Pizza Palace. "Where do you work?"

"My uncle Joe's hardware store. I make some deliveries for him after school."

"That sounds like fun," I said.

"Not really." He stopped at a classroom. "This is my class."

"Okay. See ya around." I turned and hiked my backpack higher up on one shoulder.

"Hey," he called.

I looked back over my shoulder.

"Maybe double P another day?"

"Sure," I said.

On the bad side, I might be haunted, but on the good side, I was pretty sure Nick Wesley just asked me out for pizza.

* chapter sixteen *
LEADING MAN

AS I WALKED TO THE FRONT DOOR, JIM yelled from the roof, "Hey, Sydney!"

"What?"

"Can you bring me the box of nails?"

I saw a box on the ground and climbed up the metal ladder. "Here you go," I said, and handed the box to Jim.

"Thanks, honey," he said. He wiped his nose on his gloved hand. He was sweating under his knit cap, and his cheeks were rosy. This was a whole new look for Jim Mackenzie, Sporting Goods Store Maven. "How are you? How was school?"

"I'm good, Jim."

He looked up from the nail's target with a look that said, *Don't call me Jim*, grabbed a nail, held it in place, then gave it a whack with the hammer. "I left you a list of chores on the table."

"That was thoughtful of you."

He held up a talk-to-the-hand hand. "Just do it." He whacked again, hitting the roof and missing the nail.

"Are you going to be okay up here? Should I get Cork?"

"I'm fine," he said. "Rome wasn't built in a day, you know?"

"Okay. Just be careful. I think that guy had help and had built other stuff before Rome."

That got a smile.

I stepped down the ladder, one rung at a time.

Jim called after me. "This weekend we'll start on the basement. You can help." At that the outside house lights right next to me blinked on and off, and I lost my footing and slipped. My hand slid down the metal rail, and I was going down, butt first.

"Ahhhh!" I yelled as I fell. Suddenly something broke my fall. My feet were still on the ladder, and someone had caught me at my armpits. My butt was suspended in midair over a puddle of mud. I righted myself and turned, expecting to see Elliott, but instead saw dark blue eyes.

chapter seventeen

CHORES

"YOU OKAY?" NICK ASKED.

"Yeah." I straightened my jacket. "You saved my butt. Literally." I indicated the mud and laughed. "Those lights blinked and distracted me."

"They aren't blinking now."

"No. They aren't." Then I asked, "I thought you were working today?"

"I am." He held up a brown paper bag. "Special delivery. Hooks, drill bits, lightbulbs, and electrical tape for Jim Mackenzie."

"Do you have a hanger, a driller, and an electrician in there too?" I asked.

He laughed. "I heard he was having some trouble."

"You did?"

"It's tough to keep anything quiet around this

small town. I'm sure my uncle Joe could help him out, if he needs it. He's real good at this stuff."

"I don't think he'll ask for help." I hugged myself and rubbed my arms. It was cold around here all the time. "You want some cocoa?" I asked.

"If it's the same as yesterday, yes."

He followed me into the house. "I just got home from school, how did you get here so fast?" I asked.

"I took Goog," he said. We went into the kitchen.

I got two mugs out of the cabinet. "Is that a horse or donkey?"

"Neither. Just because this isn't a big city doesn't mean we all have farm animals."

I thought I'd offended him. "Oh, right."

"Goog is an old snowmobile that me and my dad rebuilt. There's a path up the hill. I use her for deliveries sometimes." I poured two mugs of the steamy brown cream. It looked and smelled awesome. I was beginning to like Joyce's hot cocoa as much as frozen yogurt. "It beats walking up that hill," he said.

"I bet." I handed him the mug and blew on mine. He sipped. "Ouch!"

"That's why they call it *hot*."

"I guess."

I asked, "Want some whipped cream?"

"Sure," Nick said.

I looked in the fridge but didn't see any. "That's funny; I know we had some because Joyce, the woman who works here, put it on mine the other day."

He looked over my head. "It's right there."

I still couldn't find the can.

He came up behind me and reached around into the fridge. He was so close to me that I could smell chocolate on his breath. He picked up a silver bowl with a spoon sticking out. "Right here."

We came out of the fridge. "I've only ever seen it in a can."

He put a dollop on his cocoa and then mine. He sipped. "This is how we country folk like it," he said. He had a mustache of white foam. "Perfect."

I sipped. "Mmmm. It *is* perfect." I looked at his eyes again, like a movie close-up. They were really pretty.

"I know you didn't make the whipped cream, but did you make the cocoa?"

I laughed for only a second when I realized he was serious. "No. I don't know how to cook."

"Really? Nothing?"

"Nada." I sipped. "But this is good enough to make me want to learn."

"So," he said, "are you excited about your séance party Friday night?"

"Heck yeah! Why wouldn't I be?"

"I don't know. I just got the feeling maybe you were afraid to find out if you had a ghost," he said.

"Oh, no. I'm totally psyched to wake the dead, aren't you? Or are you afraid something freaky might happen . . . something like . . . I don't know . . . zombies coming out of the ground and trying to find a living body to steal? Or . . . I don't know . . . something like a vampire sucking all our blood? Is that the kind of thing you think might happen?"

He looked at me like *I* was a zombie. "No. Actually, I hadn't thought of any of that. You really do go to a lot of movies, don't you?"

"I guess I do. Actually, I really miss them."

"It's a bummer we don't have a movie theater close by," he said.

"What kind of movies do you like?"

"All different kinds, I guess."

I was excited to hear that he liked movies too.

He changed the subject. "What are these chores you have to do?"

I said, "Jim said he left me a list." I looked across the table. "There it is."

"Why do you call him Jim?"

"Ummm," I said. "I guess because that's his name."

He nodded, but I could tell he didn't get it. It was tough to explain—I'd started calling them Roz and Jim and sort of just never stopped.

I got the paper. It said:

LIST FOR SYDNEY
1. SCOOP ASHES OUT OF THE FIREPLACE
   IN THE PARLOR.
2. GATHER ALL THE DEAD FLOWERS FROM
   TOMBSTONES.
3. TAKE THE BOXES IN THE UPSTAIRS
   HALLWAY INTO THE ATTIC.
4. FILE THE STACK OF PAPERS JOYCE
   LEFT IN THE OFFICE ACCORDING TO
   HER INSTRUCTIONS.
5. SWEEP THE WORKROOM.

"That doesn't look so bad," Nick said.

I gave him a look that said, *Maybe for someone who does chores.*

"Come on, Mac." *He called me Mac!* "It's really not that bad."

Nick clearly didn't understand me. I had never had chores before.

"Look: Scoop ashes out of the fireplace," he said. "That's easy."

Maybe he thought it was easy, but I had no idea where to start.

"I'll show you how. But you're doing it yourself."

I asked, "Don't you have to get back to work?" Not because I didn't want to hang out with him, but because I didn't want him to get into trouble because of me.

"This delivery was all my uncle had for me today." He looked at the list. "You'll need a bucket, a broom and a shovel, a rag, and maybe a vacuum cleaner."

I led him to the workroom. "*Voila.* Work stuff."

He crossed his arms as if to say, *These aren't my chores.*

I picked up the bucket, shovel, and broom. I couldn't hold anything else, so he got a rag and followed me.

I stared at the fireplace.

He said, "You need to open the doors."

I did. He talked me through the cleaning, which resulted in both of us being lightly coated in ash. . . .

Okay, so maybe Nick wasn't *lightly* coated. He took the sleeve of his flannel shirt and wiped the ash off his eyes.

"Now I know what chicken feels like when it's Shake 'n Baked," he said, and laughed.

I laughed too, even though I'd never had Shake 'n Bake. But I'd heard of it.

When we were done, Nick suggested, "Maybe you should just leave the bucket of ashes in the workroom and ask your dad, errr . . . Jim, where he wants you to dump 'em."

"All right." I took out the list. "Flowers."

"Cool, the graveyard. You're gonna need a trash bag for the dead flowers." Nick pulled one out of a box in the workroom and darted out back. I was glad he was helping me.

Nick ran around looking at headstones and telling me about them. I tried hard not to be creeped out that he was walking on dead people.

We were mostly done with my list of chores when we heard Jim calling from the roof.

"What's up?" I yelled outside to him.

"Ummm," he says. "I have a little problem."

"Want me to get Roz or Cork?"

"Nah, don't do that," he called back down.

I looked at Nick, confused.

"I'll check it out." He started up the ladder. "Maybe I can help him." Once he made it to the top, I heard him and Jim talk in muffled voices.

"What is it?" I called up.

Nick gave me the *one minute* finger and disappeared onto the roof. I climbed up the ladder to see what was going on. Nick had fetched a hammer and was prying a nail out of the roof that had gone through Jim's coat before going through the shingle. Jim had nailed himself to the roof. I held back a laugh. Nick pushed hard on the handle of the hammer, and slowly the nail eased out.

Jim said, "Thanks, you're a good kid."

"You're welcome, sir."

I backed down the ladder and Nick followed, but before his head dropped below the roofline I heard Jim say, "Um, you don't have to tell anyone about this."

"No, sir," Nick said.

When he reached the bottom, the two of us covered our mouths and laughed.

Then Nick hopped on to Goog and asked, "So, do you think this place is really haunted?"

"I guess we'll find out Friday."

He zippered his coat. "I thought maybe, you know—"

"No. I don't know."

"Maybe you were making it up."

"Why would I do that?"

"To have friends. Like with the credit card in California."

I choked back a growing tear and watched Nick ride down the snowy hill.

This place had better be haunted.

* chapter eighteen *
GIRL POW

THE THUDS DIDN'T HAPPEN THE NEXT TWO nights. Maybe I *had* made it up.

I was dressed in what I thought was a good séance outfit: black sweater, black scarf, and black jeans. I laid out chips and candy. Joyce had heated up a pot of her famous hot cocoa. At ten after eight no one had arrived.

I paced in the foyer of the Victorian.

What if they were the ones who had been faking, and they really didn't think the cemetery was cool?

Headlights came up the hill into the driveway.

Phew.

Mel and Johanna hopped out of a truck and waved to the driver, who went back down the hill. I opened the front door. "Hi, guys," I said.

"What's with you?" Mel asked me. "You look like you've seen a ghost."

Johanna said, "No way! Was the spirit already here? Where was it? Inside or outside? Did we miss it? That's great—my idiot brother, Alan, couldn't find his keys, and now we missed the ghost. Didn't we?"

"No. Johanna, you didn't miss any ghosts. I was just thinking that maybe you guys had changed your minds about the séance, that's all."

"Are you KIDDING?" she yelled. "I've been working on this for two days, lots of research and practicing. I chanted all night."

Mel said, "This is the most exciting thing going on around here in a long time."

"Yeah," Johanna said. "Even more exciting than the time Nick's uncle's horse broke through the ice. Remember that, Mel?"

"Uh-huh. That *was* exciting."

To me Johanna said, "They saved the horse, but it took hours."

I said, "Speaking of Nick, where is he?"

Mel said, "I saw him after seventh period. Travis's dad got them tickets to NASCAR, and there was no way they were going to miss it."

"Oh." I was surprised Nick hadn't found me at school to tell me.

"You look bummed," Johanna said. "Wait. Press the pause button on the séance. Mac, do you like Nick Wesley?"

"No. Oh, no. It's no big deal," I said. "It will be a girls' night."

Johanna made a fist and held it up over her head and exclaimed, "Girl Pow!"

"Girl Pow?" I asked.

"Like 'Girls Rule,'" she said. Then she made the fist again and held it over her head.

Mel put a fist over her head in a mocking way. "What's this about?"

"I made it up. Just now. Cool, huh? We can do that to each other like a sign. Just for girls."

I said, "Sounds good to me." I put a fist over my head. "Girl Pow."

We looked at Mel to see her do it too, but she didn't. She just rolled her eyes and said, "Oookaay."

"I guess it's stupid." The smile faded from Johanna's face, and she started talking about the boys as if Mel pooping on her idea didn't bother her. "Seriously," she said, "we'll be better off without them. They don't believe I can do this, and I don't need anyone's negative energy hanging around. We need only positive spiritual energy and pure intentions to call the spirits." Johanna sounded like she was reading or quoting from a book. "We don't want any disruptions when I contact the *other side*."

"Huh?" Mel smooshed Johanna's face in between her hands. "Who are you and what have you done with our JoJo?"

"Stop that." Johanna pushed her hands down. "I've been doing a lot of reading about communication with spirits. Not just books, I went on the Internet, too. Plus, I talked to my aunt Pam. She thinks she's clairvoyant. She gave me tips. I can totally do this. For real. The boys wouldn't take this seriously, and that would ruin it. I can just imagine connecting with a spirit only for Travis to rip a fart."

Mel and I laughed because Johanna was so right.

"Come on. Let's go out back," Johanna said.

"You know, it's really cold out tonight. I've got some good snacks. Maybe we could just do it right here, in the kitchen . . . ," I suggested. *With the lights on.*

"Inside?" Johanna asked like that was a crazy idea. "Have you looked out back? That's a *graveyard!* That's the *perfect* place for a séance. You can't ask for better conditions than that. You must love living here."

Mel said, "Wait, are you scared?"

"No. I'm totally used to this." If I were Pinocchio, my nose would've reached the Hollywood sign. "And I do love living here."

Mel looked like she wanted to say *Yeah, right.*

I said, "Here's the thing: I didn't want to scare you, but I've seen a lot of movies, and usually a town gets taken over by zombies after a séance. So, there's that."

"And we all know that everything you see in the movies is real," Mel said sarcastically. "Jo, we better be careful of zombies."

"Yup. Sure, things can go wrong. I read about it. But that's where you're lucky."

"How am I lucky?" I asked.

"You have *me*." Johanna touched her chest. "I'm like a professional. If it looks like the spirit is getting angry at the house or that one of the twins could become possessed, I'll just pull the plug."

"Our very own zombie whisperer," Mel said. "Then we're all set. Grab the candy, and let's go out back."

This was really happening. We'd know soon enough if I'd be the haunted Gigi of Buttermilk River Cove or the outcast who made it up and now has lunch with the booger-eater table.

chapter nineteen

SÉANCE

ONE STEP INTO THE DARK CEMETERY AND I WAS instantly chilled through to my bones. Mel took the food bowls so I could slide on gloves and a hat. She bent her neck down, reached her mouth into the bowl, and ate a chip. I took Johanna's bag while she put on her hat. It was heavy. "Holy Magoo, what have you got in here?"

Mel stopped walking. "Holy Magoo? What the heck kind of dork-infested language is that?"

I explained where Magoo came from.

"It's kind of a dumb word," I said.

Mel didn't disagree, but Johanna said, "I like Magoo. It's very gooey Magooey."

The way she used the word wasn't right, but I was glad she liked it. I asked her again, "What's in this bag? Rocks?"

"Supplies," she said. "Everything we need for a successful séance. I had to go to two stores, my attic, the school lab, and Mel's shed to gather all this Magoo. I was thinking I could Magoo a séance kit and sell it on eBay. It would save Magoos a lot of time."

She was Magooing it all wrong. "That's a neat idea," I said.

"You were in my shed?" Mel asked.

"Just for a piece of flat wood. You've got a huge pile of it. I'll Magoo it back when we're done."

"Okay!" Mel said. "Let's drop the Magoo—whatcha say?"

I agreed with Mel, but the way she said it wasn't nice to the whole concept of Magoo.

"Sure," Johanna said, like Mel had just taken away her last chicken spread.

I took a flashlight out of my pocket and turned it on. Our feet crunched on the hard, frozen ground. I led us around the back of the Dolan mausoleum where Johanna laid the piece of wood she'd taken from Mel's shed. The board had writing on it.

"You were going to give it back after you wrote on it?" Mel asked.

Johanna said, "It's still wood. It can be burned."

I asked, "What are those letters?"

"That's the alphabet. This is called a weegee board. It's spelled o-u-i-j-a." She pointed to the alphabet on the top of the board. "This is how the spirits will communicate with us. We'll ask them a question, and they'll answer with letters."

"Why did you make it? Don't they sell them?" I asked.

"In Buttermilk River Cove? They don't sell much around here besides hardware, pizza (ninth slice free), army stuff, and gasoline."

"And," I added, "burial plots (tenth burial free)."

They giggled.

Mel asked, "How will the spirits tell us what letter?"

Johanna reached into her Mary Poppins bag again and took out a tinfoil triangle on top of three Q-tips that were broken in half. She set the triangle on the board, cotton balls down, like a little table. I noticed she had cut a circle out of the middle of the tinfoil triangle. She put the triangle on the letter *J* so that we could see it through the circle. "Like this. See?"

"That little Q-tip table is going to slide across the board and land on letters and spell words?" I didn't believe it.

"Yup. We're each going to put our fingers on one side of the triangle, and the spirit will guide it to a letter through our body's energy. But you have to promise not to push it. The letters have to be from the spirits," she said. "Promise me."

"I promise," I said.

She held up my hand, folded my pinkie and thumb together across my palm, and straightened up my three middle fingers. "Say, 'I swear not to move the little Q-tip table.'"

"I swear not to move the little Q-tip table," I repeated.

"And if I do, I'll kiss Mrs. Murphy's cow on the mouth."

"Gross. No way. I'm not saying that. I'm not kissing any cow."

"If you don't push the table, you don't have anything to worry about," Johanna said.

Mel added, "Just swear. I've seen her like this before. She's a stubborn Magoo."

Maybe Mel didn't think it was dumb after all.

"Fine." I rolled my eyes and repeated the pledge. Then I looked at Mel, who was checking out the Ouija board. "Don't you have to swear?" I asked her.

Johanna said, "It wouldn't do any good. If she

wanted to move it, she'd do it anyway. I've seen her kiss a cow; she doesn't care."

"Yuck," I said.

"It wasn't pretty," Johanna said.

"Then make her swear something else. Something grosser, if there is such a thing."

"Enough about kissing cows." Mel tossed a fistful of Sour Patch Kids into her mouth. "Let's get this séance started. What do we do, JoJo?"

"Okay, first we take this sea salt." She pulled a shaker out of the sack. "And make a white circle around us by sprinkling it on the ground."

Mel took the salt. I guided her in a circle with a flashlight. "What's that for?" I asked.

Johanna took a note card out of the back pocket of her jeans and read it. "It protects us if we release a wicked soul or something, I guess."

"You guess?" I didn't like the sound of that. "Great," I said. "Good to have a circle of salt if we're attacked by the wicked or something."

"I don't think it'll happen, but I don't want to take a chance." She was serious, while I had been sarcastic.

"Done," Mel said.

Johanna put the salt away and took out a tall white

pillar candle and matches. "Light this and set it on the north side of us."

"Which way is that?" I asked.

She produced a compass. Seriously, she had a compass. She wasn't kidding about being like a professional. But being *like* a professional wasn't the same as *being* a professional—someone with séance experience, like an old lady who's been talking to the dead for fifty years. *That's* the kind of person we needed. Johanna looked at the compass. "That side is north."

"And what's the candle for?" Mel asked.

"I think it's so that the spirits can see us." She shoved the index card back in her pocket. "I guess being dead and all, sometimes they can't see real clearly. That makes sense when you think about it. They don't have glasses or eye doctors on the other side."

"Yup," I said. It actually did kind of make sense. But I didn't like that we were guessing about things. Mel and I dug a little hole for the candle and lit it. It flickered in the cold night air, but it didn't go out.

Next, Johanna pulled out a jug of water. She took the cap off and took a big swig. She handed it to

Mel, who took a drink and handed it to me. "Purifi-cation," she said without us asking. "And hydration."

I didn't ask for any details since she seemed pretty sure about this one.

"Okay. We have to hold hands."

Johanna closed her eyes and breathed in really deeply and dramatically. She was totally serious about this.

"Close your eyes," she said.

I did what she said. "You got this from a book?" I asked.

"Books, plural," Johanna said. "Now, shhh."

Oh, well, I guess that makes you like a professional.

chapter twenty

CALLING THE SPIRIT

WE WERE ALL REALLY QUIET FOR A FEW SECONDS.

"Clear. Your. Miiiiind," Johanna said in a low, quiet, and drawn-out voice that reminded me of *I vaaant to suuuck your blooood*. A chill went up my back. "We are calling to the spirit that has been haunting Lay to Rest Cemetery."

There was no response.

"We come in peace," Johanna said in her séance voice.

Mel asked, "Isn't that what the Pilgrims said to the Indians?"

"Shh," Johanna said. "Be serious or no one is going to answer us."

A little louder she called out, "We would like to talk to the spirit who has been haunting Lay to Rest

Cemetery. Please come to us tonight." Then in her regular voice she softly said to us, "Okay, open your eyes. Put your fingers on the triangle, but rest them very, very lightly so that it can move under us. You can't push it, and you can't put the weight of your fingers on it."

We put the tips of our gloved fingers on the foil.

"Now I'm going to ask questions." I could see her breath coming out in puffs in the cold. She changed her voice again. "Spirit of the cemetery, are you with ussss? If you are among us, make yourself known."

The wind blew in the trees. Johanna waited, then chanted. "Was that yooouuu, spirit, or just the wind blowing when I asked you that question?"

No answer. "Spirit, if you are among us, show us a sign." The wind blew harder, blowing out the candle.

I jumped. My heart rate sped up.

I thought I heard a rustle in the woods on one side of the cemetery.

"What was that?" I asked. "Did you hear that?"

"Shh," Johanna said. "Are you the spirit who has been haunting the cemetery?"

I couldn't believe what I was feeling, but the tin-foil triangle on Q-tips was moving under my fingers.

It was gliding across the wood. It went to the letter *Y*. Then slowly it went to *E*. Then to *S*.

I gulped. This was totally scary.

I looked at Mel suspiciously. "Was that you?"

She shook her head, but I didn't believe her. I gave her a questioning head tilt like, *Come on, tell the truth*. She whispered, "Seriously. If I'm lying, I'll kiss a cow's butt."

I thought about this and looked at Johanna. "Have you ever seen her do *that*?"

"No. I've seen her kiss a cow, Travis, and a duck, but all were on the face or head or beak. The butt would be new."

"You kissed Travis?" I whispered.

"Yeah," Mel said. She took in a breath like she was going to tell me the story about the kiss when Johanna interrupted.

"Not now. Mel, did you move the triangle or not?"

"NOT!"

Phew. So there is a haunting. I'm not a liar and still have friends. I should feel "yay!" but, you know, now there's a ghost and all.

"Fine. Then let's continue," Johanna said. "Spirit. Tell us your name."

The triangle moved to *I*. A cloud blew in front of the gray moon, hiding any natural light we had.

There was another rustle in the woods. It was louder this time.

"You heard that? Didn't you?" I asked.

Mel said, "I did."

The triangle moved some more. It moved to *V*.

Then I felt a little stone hit me in the back. "Ouch!" I cried, and I took my hands off the table. Then a stone landed on the board. Another hit the water jug. Another hit Mel in the head. They were all coming from the direction of the woods. Mel tried to run out, but Johanna pulled her back inside the sea-salt circle.

"Where are you going?" I asked her. "Are you crazy? It could be a wicked spirit."

"Someone hit me with a stone. I'm gonna kick some butt."

"Someone? Or some*thing*?" Johanna asked.

"You aren't a Ghostbuster," I said to Mel. "You're a mere mortal. You can't kick a ghost's butt. Geez, I knew this was a bad idea. Now we've opened a portal to the other side! All kinds of evil can slip through into our world."

Mel snorted. "Portal? Come on. Are you for real?"

Then we heard a noise. Not any kind of ghostly howl or cry. It was a laugh. A human laugh.

"I know that sound." Mel pulled away from Johanna and crossed the salt circle. She ran straight for the woods.

There was more laughter—eighth-grade-boy-style laughter.

Mel said, "They're gonna get it."

Johanna grabbed the flashlight. "Come on. We have to save them."

"You should let her get them for scaring us like that." Then I added, "What about the portal? You can't just walk away and leave it open."

Johanna set both palms on the board and said, "I pronounce this séance session closed." I thought her next line was going to be *You may now kiss the bride*. She pulled me by the arm. "Just come on. I don't want her to go to prison at such a young age."

I followed Johanna into the woods where Mel had tackled Travis. She was smacking him in the head. Nick couldn't help him because he was laughing too hard. We pulled Mel off and possibly saved Travis's life.

chapter twenty-one

THE SECRET IN THE WOODS

TRAVIS WAS BENT OVER WITH LAUGHTER about how they'd scared us. I was too mad to think it was funny.

"You jerk!" Johanna said, and swatted at Nick, making Travis laugh harder. So she tossed a few kicks his way.

Mel laughed at Johanna beating up Travis.

I crossed my arms across my chest. "That was mean," I said. I was serious, and when Nick caught my eye, he knew I meant it. He stopped laughing, but Travis was clueless.

Mel said, "Lighten up. It was a joke."

No one had ever told me to lighten up.

Nick looked at me, and I could tell that he knew that what Mel had said bothered me. "Oh, we have something so cool to show you." He swung his hand against mine in a come-with-me way.

"You want us to follow you into the woods? How do we know it's not another trick?" I asked.

Mel followed Nick and looked at me. "You don't. That's the excitement! This is how we have fun around here. Come on, Syd." She didn't have to coax Johanna.

The four of them walked away from me.

Travis wiped tears of laughter out of the corners of his eyes and said, "You're gonna love this."

I had a choice:

Stay here all alone in the dark woods next to the cemetery without so much as a flashlight or sea salt, where it was quite possible that an evil ghost had recently slipped through a portal from the spirit world to ours.

Or:

Trust my four new friends, two of whom had just played a huge joke on me that was not funny, and two who had just communicated with the dead, and follow them deeper into the dark woods next to a cemetery, where it was quite possible that an evil ghost had recently slipped through a portal from the spirit world to ours. Remember, they had the flashlight and sea salt—although we only "guessed" that the salt protected us from the wicked; we were not actually sure.

What to do?

Nick turned back to me. "You coming?" His eyes were oh so cute.

Nearby leaves crackled, making me jump out of my skin. I ran to catch up to the flashlights in front of me.

"What is it?" Mel asked Travis.

"If I tell you, it will spoil the surprise," Travis said. "But it's gonna be good."

"Is it alive?" Johanna asked.

"Nope," Nick said.

Great, then it's dead.

Johanna asked, "Is it a skeleton? A skull? Oh my God, you've found human remains, haven't you? A femur? A rib?"

"You need to lay off the TV," Travis said.

Mel said, "Because there's sooo much other stuff to do around here."

Nick said, "We're almost there."

"What happened to NASCAR?" I asked.

"A fart," Travis said.

"A fart?" Mel asked.

"A *farce*," Nick said. "He means a farce. They kinda rhyme, but mean very different things."

"We made up the NASCAR thing," Travis said. "So we could SCARE YOU!" He yelled "scare you" so close to me that he made me jump again.

We walked for another minute without talking.

Nick stopped. He shined his flashlight at a huge clump of weeds at the base of a small incline. "There it is."

"What is it?" I asked.

"What do you mean 'what is it'? Can't you see?" Travis asked like he was offended that I didn't immediately appreciate their amazing finding.

Mel stepped closer and stretched her neck to get a closer look. "A cave? Why would there be a cave out here?"

I said, "Maybe it's a bear den."

"Huh, I hadn't thought of a bear den," Nick said.

Johanna said, "Or it could be for dragons or crocodiles."

I liked her ideas more than mine, because I imagined a werewolf home.

"But it's better than just your plain old everyday cave," Travis said.

We didn't understand so he gave us clues. "Rhymes with funnel . . . and it starts with a *t*."

"A tunnel!" we yelled.

"I'd heard that there were tunnels in town, but I didn't believe it," Nick said.

"How do you know that?" Travis asked.

"Someone pays attention in school," Mel said.

Nick said, "VanOstrum told us that the Underground Railroad went through Buttermilk River Cove."

Johanna said, "I don't see any railroad tracks."

Nick said, "It wasn't really a railroad. And actually, it wasn't really underground. But I guess this part was."

Johanna asked, "Where do you think it goes?"

"Only one way to find out," Mel said. "Go ahead, boys. Check it out and let us know what you find."

"Um," I said. "Is that a good idea? What if the roof crumbles in?"

The boys hesitated.

"Mac might be right," Travis said.

Mel put her hands under her armpits and flapped her elbows up and down. "Bawk! Bawk, bawk!"

Nick started into the tunnel. "If we hear a bear snoring, or see the ceiling start to collapse, we'll come right back out."

With that, they vanished into the dark hole.

chapter twenty-two

TUNNEL

JOHANNA, MEL, AND I FOUND A BOULDER not too far from the tunnel entrance where we planted our butts and waited for the boys to come out. It was cold. We sat real close, trying to share our body heat.

"They're crazy," I said.

Mel said, "They'll be fine. Nothing exciting ever happens in Buttermilk River Cove. Believe me. No yeti, no cave-in. The only exciting thing I can think of was the time the horse fell through the ice."

I said, "You already told me about that."

"See," Jo said. "That's all we got."

I said, "I guess it is pretty boring. You don't even have a movie theater."

"Boring? You think it's boring here because it's not

like Hollywood?" Mel asked. "Sorry we're so boring for you."

I did it again. I forgot that it was okay for her to think Buttermilk River Cove was boring but not me.

"I didn't really mean *boring*," I said. "Actually a séance in the middle of a graveyard is exciting, right?"

"Right," Johanna said.

"And finding a secret tunnel hidden in the woods is exciting," I said. "I've never done that before."

"Me neither," Johanna said.

Mel was still silent.

"And living in this amazing cemetery in a haunted house is . . . well . . . it's *amazing*. So maybe there's no movie theater. So what? Actually, this place is anything but boring."

I waited for Mel's reaction.

"I guess," Mel said. "Maybe things are changing."

"Maybe," I said. "JoJo can really talk to the dead. Nick and Travis could run out of that tunnel being chased by a phantom or a creature from the center of the earth."

Mel said, "*That* would be exciting."

Johanna added, "Or the tunnel will collapse, and we'll have to stick pipes in the ground to talk to them and give them air. And the National Guard will come up to the top of this hill to dig them out, and we'll be on the news."

"Now, *that* would be cool," Mel said.

"Except it would mean that Nick and Travis would be trapped in an underground tunnel," I pointed out.

"Right," Johanna said. "That part probably wouldn't be good."

I wiggled my butt cheeks, which were starting to freeze onto the boulder, and I thought back to the board. "What do you think *I-V* is?" I asked.

Johanna said, "I was thinking it's IV, like in a hospital when the doctor puts a tube in someone's arm and the liquid goes in."

I asked, "What does that kind of IV have to do with a spirit or a haunting?"

"Maybe he has one stuck in his arm and needs help getting it out. Like that fairy tale about the lion with a thorn in his foot. And the brave mouse pulls it out and they become best friends. Maybe the spirit needs us to pull the IV out."

I didn't think that was right, but it was interesting to see how her mind worked.

"That's possible," I said. "But I was thinking maybe it's the beginning of a name, like Ivan, or Ivanna, or . . . or it could be a last name."

The wind blew the bare tree limbs overhead. A chill went up my back that felt like more than just cold temperature. I didn't want to talk about ghosts anymore. "So, tell me about the time you kissed Travis."

"Ooooo," Johanna said. "Tell her, tell her."

"It was nothing. It was on a dare. And I have a policy never to turn down a dare."

"She does," Johanna confirmed.

"Who dared you?"

"Me!" Johanna raised her hand. "She won't admit it, but I think she's had a secret crush on Travis for like a year."

I asked Mel, "Do you?"

"No!"

"Why would she keep it a secret from you?" I asked Johanna. "I mean, wouldn't you guys talk about stuff like that? You know, like make a plan to see him or something."

Johanna said, "I guess so. I used to think Michael Finnegan was cute, and we followed him everywhere. One time we even pretended there was free pizza at the Pizza Palace just so we could hang out with him. Remember, Mel?"

"I remember." Then she added, "Look, I don't have a thing for Travis."

Yes, she does, Johanna mouthed to me.

"What happened to Michael Finnegan?" I asked.

"Oh, he's still around. He plays hockey."

There was a rustle in the woods. Johanna shined her flashlight toward it. A bird flew out of its beam.

"They've been gone awhile," I said. "You think they're all right?"

Johanna said, "It has been kind of a long time."

"Let's give 'em a shout," Mel said.

We walked to the entrance to the tunnel, which from here looked more like a cave. Mel pulled aside some branches that blocked the entrance. Johanna shined the flashlight in the hole while Mel cupped her hands around her mouth. "Hey, guys! What are you doing?"

No answer.

"Travis!"

No answer.

"Nick!"

No answer.

Mel said, "I bet they're right here around us, hiding. Just getting ready for the chance to scare us again."

I looked around in the dark but only saw darkness.

We crept around the area and didn't see anything.

"Maybe they went back to the house, and they're sitting at your kitchen table right now, sipping hot cocoa and laughing that we're out here in the cold," Johanna said.

"Probably. Come on—let's go up there and give them a piece of our minds," Mel said. "I'm getting frostbite."

We went to the site of the séance and gathered Johanna's supplies. Then we entered the Victorian through the workroom door, took off our muddy boots, and went into the kitchen.

No boys.

We ladled cocoa into mugs, cupped our cold hands around them, and sat down. "What do you think we should do?" I asked. "It's ten o'clock. Maybe we should call the police or something."

"Call Sheriff Wesley and tell him that we lost his son and Travis in a hidden tunnel under the cemetery?" Johanna asked.

"I don't think I wanna make that call," Mel said.

"Let's give them fifteen more minutes," I suggested.

"And you said nothing ever happens in Buttermilk River Cove," Johanna said to Mel. "I think Nick and Travis really might be lost."

That's when we heard a noise.

chapter twenty-three

SOMETHIN' SOMETHIN' IN THE BASEMENT

I JUMPED. "WHAT WAS THAT?"

Mel said, "I didn't hear anything."

"I did," Johanna said. "It was like a knocking, or banging."

It happened again.

"Did you hear *that*?" I asked.

Mel's eyes bulged.

I asked, "Do you think a spirit is trying to get in the house?"

"I think they can float through walls," Johanna said. "But if that's what's happening, we're at a whole new level of haunting."

It happened again.

And again.

And again.

Knocking.

Mel said, "Sounds like it's coming from down-stairs. Do you have a basement?"

"Sort of."

Johanna asked, "What's down there?"

I just looked at them because the words wouldn't come out.

"What's down there, Mac?" Mel asked.

"It's where we keep the . . . the ummm . . . err . . ."

"WHAT?" Johanna asked, but I couldn't get the words out.

"The dead bodies?" Mel asked. "Please say it's bodies."

All I could do was nod. I felt the color leave my face.

Mel's face lit up. "Are there any down there right now?"

"I don't think so. But I haven't been down there."

Johanna asked, "Well, have any been delivered?"

"Not that I know of," I said. "I don't think they just show up on your doorstep like a package from UPS."

"Maybe Uncle Ted left you a little extra somethin' down there before he kicked the bucket," Mel said. "And then our little séance called it back to life!"

"Do you think I could do that? What am I saying? I could totally do that! I've been reading about this stuff for two days. But it could be that he was never really dead, like John Hancock."

"Or," I said softly, "he's *un*dead." The words made my entire body shiver.

An eerie quiet filled the room as we thought about these possibilities. The silence was interrupted by more knocking.

"Let's check it out," Mel said.

"Maybe we should wake up Elliott," I said.

"To tell him we had a séance and opened a portal and there could be a spirit in your basement right now?" Mel asked. "Sure. Go for it. Let me know how that works out for you."

I shrugged because she was right—it sounded crazy.

"It's decided then," Mel said. "We're going down."

I didn't remember deciding on that.

Mel opened the basement door and flicked the wall light switch, but it turned on a light in the hallway behind us.

"Pretty typical," Johanna said.

"What do you mean?" I asked.

"You can have electrical issues without a ghost,

but if you have a ghost, then you will definitely have electrical problems." She went back to the kitchen table to get the flashlight, and shined it at the bottom of the stairs. I remembered Elliott and Joyce talking the other day. They said it was happening "again." So either Lay to Rest had been haunted before, or I-V had been lingering around the cemetery and Victorian for a long time.

Mel took the flashlight. We followed her down the steps. At the bottom she shined the light all around. There was a stainless-steel table, the kind that a body would go on. It was shiny and clean, and unoccupied. The floor was cement, and there was a clean drain in the center.

No sign of a corpse, zombie, or spirit.

I felt something brush against my shoulder. I swung at it, thinking it was a spider web or the fingers of a phantom. But it was an ordinary string. I pulled it.

And the room was filled with light. I looked at Johanna for an explanation. "Hauntings don't mess up every single light," she said.

Then the knocking started again.

chapter twenty-four

THE SECRET ROOM

WE LOOKED AT THE WALL WHERE THE SOUND was coming from. There was a workbench covered with towels and toolboxes. For just a second I wondered what kinds of tools would be needed down here with a dead body, but then I didn't want to think about it.

Mel stepped closer to the wall. For the first time since I met her, she actually seemed a little nervous.

Johanna and I were still hanging on to each other as we stepped closer. Every inch of my body was covered in goose bumps.

"Help me slide this," Mel said, indicating the table.

"Why? Whatever is on the other side of that wall might try to break through," I said.

Mel reached over the table and knocked a rhythm

on the wall. It was a beat that needed two more knocks to be complete. A reply came from the other side of the wall—*knock knock*—finishing the pattern.

"I know what's behind there," Mel said. "And believe me, I don't want to let it out either."

Johanna asked, "How do you know? If one of us is suddenly psychic, it should be *me*."

Mel got to one end of the table. "Unfortunately, we have to let it out. Push this table with me."

I hoped she knew what she was doing. We pushed the workbench, and behind it was a low door. It was small, like it went to a hidden storage compartment. The door was painted over to be the same color as the wall. With the table in front of it, it was easily unnoticeable. There was a small metal ring, also painted the same color as the wall.

Mel picked up the ring and pulled. The door didn't move.

"Maybe it's locked," I said, "to keep whatever is in there *in*." I pictured the door opening and the souls of all the dead who've ever been at Lay to Rest coming out and swooping around. Three of them would instantly take over our bodies. The rest would fly upstairs, take over Joyce, Cork, Elliott, my parents— maybe they'd miss the twins before they hit the rest of the town. Buttermilk River Cove as we knew it would cease to exist unless One and Two could save them. . . . This would make a good movie. The tagline could be: *Can two Dumb-Os save the planet?*

Mel pulled the metal ring again. "Are you sure you want to do that?" I asked.

"Yep," she grunted as she put her foot on the wall to give her more leverage on the little door.

Pop!

The door flew open and Mel fell back on the ground, hard.

Travis and Nick came out of the storage compartment, covered with dirt, dust, and cobwebs. Travis was *not* laughing. Johanna was the first person he saw. He hugged her. "Thank you. I never thought we would get out," he said. "You saved our lives." Next he hugged me, then Mel. I noticed that he hugged Mel longer than he did me and Johanna.

I hoped that Nick was going to give me a hug too, but he just sat on the floor against the wall with a serious look in his eye and a very dim flashlight in his hand. "Where are we?" he asked.

"In my basement," I said.

"That tunnel led us to your basement. Why?" he asked.

No one had an answer.

The boys dusted off. We slid the table back and went upstairs. Travis was quiet. The rest of us asked one another questions we couldn't answer:

Why was there a tunnel?

Why did it lead to the basement?

Why would people want to sneak into the Victorian from the woods?

Who dug it? When?

Was it related to the Underground Railroad?

We decided we should look on the computer to see if there was anything about tunnels and Buttermilk River Cove on the Internet. I got my laptop.

"Is that yours?" Johanna asked.

"Yeah. I had to cat-sit for the whole neighborhood for months to save up for it," I admitted, something I'd never told Leigh.

While it booted up, the guys ate cookies and sipped buttermilk cocoa. Travis was afraid that in the hour he was trapped he'd gotten dehydrated and become vitamin D deficient, and he thought chocolate chip cookies and cocoa were a good source of vitamins.

"What do I search for? 'Secret tunnels in Buttermilk River Cove, Delaware'?" I asked.

"Does this cemetery have a website?" Nick asked. "Maybe it has a history section for information like the John Hancock thing and tunnels."

The mention of John Hancock made me feel bad again about making up the story. I googled Lay to Rest Cemetery and found Uncle Ted's website. It needed serious updating. It was one page with terrible pictures of the Victorian, the address, and phone number. There were no links and no history section.

"Try tunnels," Nick suggested

I googled "Buttermilk River Cove" and "tunnels" and was scanning the hits when the phone rang. I got it before it could wake anyone up. It was Alan, Johanna's brother. I gave her the phone. She spoke for a second and hung up. "He's on his way to pick me up," she said.

I quickly summarized the information I'd found. "It says here that there were tunnels throughout Delaware in the early nineteen hundreds as a way of hiding slaves who were escaping north."

I continued, "Then, it says that since emancipation most tunnels collapsed or were filled in."

Travis said, "Well, someone forgot to fill this one in, and it should be, because it is really creepy. Do you know how scared I was? I seriously thought I was going to die. The walls were closing in. Oxygen was running out. I really thought that the last face I was going to see was this one right here." He patted Nick on the back. "My best bud. He didn't say it, but I knew he would hold me as I sucked in my last breath. When archaeologists found us in a hundred years, they would find our bones wrapped together." He looked at Nick. "Is this guy a friend, or what?"

I thought he might cry.

Nick waved him off. "You would've done the same thing for me if you weren't hyperventilating."

"Weren't you scared?" I asked Nick.

"Nah," Nick said. "I was pretty sure we'd get out eventually. But I was getting hungry." He bit a cookie.

"Are you kidding me?" Travis said. "He held my hand so tight, I thought he would squeeze it off. He said, 'If I don't make it, tell my mom I love her.'"

Nick blushed. We all laughed, and soon he was laughing at himself too.

"What was it like in there?" Johanna asked.

"Well, it was dark—very, very dark," Travis said. "And some areas were smaller than others, so small that we had to crawl." He indicated his clothes. "That's why we're so dirty."

"Why didn't you turn around and go back the way you came?" I asked.

"An excellent question!" Travis snapped. "And one I asked my best bud many times while I was deep beneath the earth's outer crust waiting to be crushed by tons of dirt and stone. And a question that I would like an answer to. Nick, best bud, please tell us. Why couldn't we just turn around, like I said a bazillion times?"

"You're going to think it's crazy," Nick said.

Mel said, "Not crazier than a ghost talking to us through a homemade Ouija board."

Travis asked, "Seriously? It worked?"

Johanna lit up with a proud smile. "It did."

Nick looked at me. "So it's real."

"Right. Not a pretend haunting," I said to Nick.

"Who would pretend about something like that?" Travis asked.

"No one," I said.

"Did the spirit tell you what it wants?" Travis asked.

"It didn't get a chance because someone was THROWING ROCKS AT US!" Johanna yelled.

"Oops," Travis said.

I turned back to Nick. "So what was so crazy that you couldn't turn around?"

"I heard something," he said.

"In the tunnel?" I asked.

"Actually, I heard it before going in. There was a sound that led us to the tunnel. That's why we found it."

Travis said, "That's right. It was like a thump."

The hairs on my arms lifted. "Or was it like a thud?"

"YES!" Travis said. "It was like a thud!"

"That's what I've heard. The ghost thuds while I'm sleeping."

"Well," Nick continued, "when we were in the tunnel, the thudding led us to your basement. But then the flashlight was dying, and I didn't want to crawl back in the dark, maybe get lost. So we banged."

"And banging on a brick wall is tough on the knuckles." Travis showed us the dried blood on the back of his hand. "I thought you said the tunnel was dirt," Johanna said.

"It was," Nick said. "Except at the end. The area near your basement was lined with brick, and the walls were rounded. It reminded me of an old brick oven."

Mel stroked an imaginary beard and thought out loud. "An oven in the basement of a cemetery house?"

"You know what?" I said, clicking on my laptop.

I opened Uncle Ted's antique website again. "Some bodies aren't buried." I pointed to one word on the screen: "crematorium."

Mel said, "That means . . ."

Nick held up his hand. "We get it. You don't need to explain."

"What?" Travis asked. "I don't get it."

Nick explained, "We were sitting in an oven where bodies were burned to ash."

chapter twenty-five

HARDY BOYS

"I WONDER IF I-V WAS CREMATED?" JOHANNA asked.

"Who?" Travis asked.

"The spirit said its name was I-V," I explained.

Travis and Nick looked at each other, and the color faded from their faces.

"What is it?" Mel asked.

Johanna asked, "Do you hear the ghost? Is it talking to you right now? Shhhh! I don't hear it."

Nick ignored her. "Or maybe," he said, "its name is Ivy, like *i-v-y*."

Travis nodded and his shoulders shimmied really fast. "That's so creepy that I just got a chill."

"What's creepy?" I asked. "Who's Ivy?"

Nick said, "That name was carved on a brick in the basement."

"You're kidding," I said.

Mel said, "We need to check that out more closely."

Johanna's eyes popped open. "Yes!"

"No way," said Travis. "No freakin' way. I'm staying right here."

Mel asked, "What do you mean no freakin' way? Don't you want to check it out?"

"No. I absolutely do *not* want to go back in there to check out a carving left by a ghost," Travis said. "That's what I mean by no freakin' way."

"Maybe it's not a good idea," I suggested.

Headlights came into the driveway of the Victorian. "Oh, bummer-fest, there's Alan," Johanna said. "I gotta go. Call me the second you find something. Who wants a ride home?"

Travis's hand jetted into the air. He shoved another cookie in his mouth and threw on his jacket. Mel tied her scarf around her neck. "I gotta go too. If I'm late again, my dad will kill me," she said. "Mac, see what you can find out about the brick and let us know."

"You coming?" Travis asked Nick.

"I'll head home in a few," Nick said. "After I look at that brick again with Sydney."

"Okay," Travis said. "But make sure the sheriff knows that this time it's not my fault if you're late."

Travis, Johanna, and Mel left.

I popped a cheese puff into my mouth. Even though I wanted to hang out with Nick, I wasn't going to climb into the crematorium and check out a brick—no way!

After the front door closed, Nick asked, "You ready?"

"Awesome," I said. "Let's go." I looked at my watch. "Unless you think it's too late. We could do it some other time. Maybe during the day would be better . . . more light."

"Wait. Are you scared? I thought you liked this stuff?"

"Oh, I do. I just thought you might be a little shaken up after being trapped in that tunnel. You know . . ." I pretended to be a talk-show host. "When you were trapped in the small dark tunnel, unsure of your direction, losing your flashlight's batteries, losing oxygen, hearing the thud of a ghost, and not knowing if you would ever get out, weren't you scared?"

Nick reached for a cheese puff. "Maybe I was a

little nervous when Travis mentioned that the walls were closing in and that he felt spiders crawling into his ears. But I kept it together, for his sake."

"What a good friend."

"Yeah, I guess. I'm pretty sure he'll have nightmares. I just hope he doesn't call me in the middle of the night to tell me about them. Sometimes being Travis O'Flynn's best bud isn't as easy as it sounds," he said. "So, do you wanna look at the brick?" He didn't wait for an answer as he walked to the basement door. "Who woulda thought our JoJo could be a . . . a . . . what would we call her? Not a fortune-teller. A ghost communicator? A spiritualist?"

"Spiritualist sounds good. That would be a good title for a movie, *The Spiritualist*, huh? Although Johanna would probably call it *The Spiritualist-Aphoner*. Which is probably too confusing for a movie title."

"You sure do like the movies."

"Yeah. It's probably what I miss most from California—movies and drama class."

"Buttermilk River Cove is about as far from the acting and the movie scene as you're gonna get," Nick said. "How about you play the part of a brave ghost hunter going into the basement of a big old Victorian house? We'll be like the Hardy Boys!"

"That would make me a boy."

"I thought you were an actress. Maybe you only play easy roles. You can't act like you're a Hardy Boy?"

"No," I said. "I can do it. I can act like a Hardy Boy like it's nobody's business."

"That's what I thought. Let's go."

chapter twenty-six

IVY'S BRICK

WE WENT DOWN THE STAIRS, MOVED THE TABLE out of the way, and opened the door. Nick shined a light inside.

"Are we under the Last Chance Room?" Nick asked.

I nodded.

"I love that story about John Hancock."

I nodded, but that felt like a punch in the belly.

"The smoke probably goes out the chimney."

I asked, "So where is this brick?"

He climbed in, then turned back to look at me. "Aren't you coming?"

"You're doing fine."

"One Hardy Boy wouldn't let another one do this alone." He held his hand out to me.

Nick sat with his back against one of the brick walls. I crossed my legs and faced the same direction.

Nick flashed the light on the bricks in front of us. It lit up a brick on which was clearly scratched *Ivy*, under which, less clearly, was etched *1825*.

I asked, "Did you see this number?"

"I didn't notice that. My flashlight battery was fading. I'd bet it's a year."

Nick touched the brick. "You know, it feels loose." He reached into his pocket and pulled out his plastic Pizza Palace club card. He wedged it between the bricks and wiggled it. "You get the ninth slice free," he said.

"Yeah, I've heard. I have to get one of those."

Nick eased the brick out of its spot, studied it. "Nothing special." He slid the brick back in, but it didn't go all the way. He pushed it harder.

"Wait," I said. "Pull that out again." I shined the flashlight into the brick's hole. I got real close and blew dust out of the way. Then I put my finger in the hole.

[Jolt of suspenseful music!]

I yelled, "Ahhhh! AHHHH!"

chapter twenty-seven

SLUDGE-KICKERS

NICK JUMPED!

He grabbed my arm and yanked until it was free from the hole.

He looked at my fingers.

"What?" he asked. "What was it? Did something grab you? Bite you?"

I opened both hands all the way to show Nick I was completely uninjured. "I just wanted to get even with you for the little trick you pulled on us in the woods." I worked hard to hold in my smile.

Nick's face remained flat.

I put my hand back in the hole and removed a piece of frayed cloth. "Here." I gave the flashlight to a sourpuss Nick. I carefully unwrapped the fabric as something shiny fell into my hands.

"It's a silver locket," I said, holding it up.

Nick and I agreed that the Hardy Boys would investigate Ivy and the locket the next afternoon. His dad picked him up in a squad car.

Saturday, Nick Wesley and I walked down Main Street. We headed toward the library, passing the police station on the way. "Is your dad there?" I asked.

"Nah. He's out investigating a cold case this week."

"What's that?"

"It's an old case that was never solved. We have a lot of them on account of Buttermilk River Cove having an ultra-small police department for most of its existence."

"What kind of cases?"

"Let's see, there was a big bank heist, a ring of forgeries, something about gold bars . . . there was even an old baby-switching case."

"So that must keep him busy," I said.

"It does. He says it's good we don't have much new crime. Only old stuff."

I avoided the puddles in my short, black leather boots with a little chunky heel.

"Any visits from Ivy last night?" he asked.

"Yeah, thuds. I thought maybe finding the locket

would make it stop. I talked to Johanna this morning. She says there's probably something I have to do with the locket before Ivy will go away."

"Well, JoJo would know." Nick walked fast through the slush. "She's read books, ya know?"

"I guess." Between my shoes and backpack, which contained a notebook and laptop, I had trouble keeping up with Nick's pace.

"I'll take that." He took my pack. I still had trouble navigating the messy sidewalk. "So, has your dad, er . . . Jim started working in the basement?"

"Soon," I said. "You know, I was thinking, if he had done that work before the roof, we would never have ever found the locket," I said.

We arrived at the army-navy store. "Then it's a good thing we found it when we did." A buzzer indicated that a customer had arrived.

"This isn't the library," I said.

"It'll only take a minute."

I was surprised to see Travis walk out from the back of the store. "Hey hey hey! What up, guys?"

"What are you doing here?" I asked.

"I work here. This is my cousin Woody's store."

"Is it me, or do everyone's relatives live and work in this town?"

"It isn't you," Travis said. "All my relatives live here. Pretty much everyone is related somehow to someone else."

"Except for Mrs. Dolan," Nick said. "Her kids moved to Philadelphia."

"Can you blame them? If everyone thought I was cursed, I'd leave town too," Travis said.

"Why are they cursed?" I asked.

"Does there have to be a reason?" Travis asked.

"I think so," I said. "You aren't just born that way, are you?"

"Maybe it's because she's a witch," Travis said.

"What does she do that's witchy?" I asked.

They looked at each other and shrugged.

"You guys don't seem to know much about this Dolan curse," I said.

"Look," Nick said. "I just know I was always told they were cursed. It has something to do with their ancestors."

"And they just *inherited* the curse? That doesn't make sense," I said.

"It seems perfectly logical to me," Travis said.

"Her kids come home for the Tomato Ball; maybe you can ask them then," Nick said.

Travis said, "Oh, that will go over really well. . . .

'Hi there. You don't know me, but why is your family cursed?'"

"What's the Tomato Ball?" I asked.

"At the end of the summer we gather up all the extra tomatoes, and we have a contest to see who can catapult one the farthest across Cattail Field. We all get dressed up—"

Travis interrupted. "Fancy, like a ball."

Nick said, "And we throw tomatoes—"

"Like balls. You know, footballs, baseballs, soft-balls, and golf balls." Travis finished Nick's sentences the way Roz did for Jim.

"And usually folks make tomato pie, tomato soup, tomato casserole, tomato sauces, and tomato salads. Mayor Margreither dresses up like a tomato. There's a DJ and a dance floor—"

"Like a ball," I said.

"It's like the ending to the summer," Nick said.

"It's one of the many highlights of Buttermilk River Cove." Travis smiled proudly. "And now we even have our very own ghost. I'm glad you made it through the night okay after we disturbed it."

"Yeah. Here I am," I said. "Tired, but here in the flesh and blood, although I almost lost an arm." I held up the hand that I had shoved into the brick hole.

"Don't ask," Nick said.

"I won't," he said. "So what's your plan?"

"We're gonna look through the town's old records and see if there was anyone named Ivy who lived around here in 1825," Nick said, and told him about the date on the brick.

"Mrs. Schuldner should know. She was probably alive then," Travis said. "What are you gonna do if you find Ivy in the records?"

I explained Johanna's theory that since Ivy was still hanging around, she probably wanted me to do something with the locket. "And maybe if we can find out who she is, we can figure out what we have to do."

"Well, good luck."

I thought we were going to leave, but Nick said, "Hey, we need a pair of sludge-kickers, size . . . What are you, Mac, a seven?"

I liked it when he called me Mac. "Six and a half."

Travis said, "You got it." He disappeared.

Nick motioned for me to sit down. "Take off your boots."

I was a little unsure what we were doing, but I unzipped the sides of my boots and took them off.

The bottom of my skinny jeans and my socks (both pairs) were wet.

Travis reappeared and gave Nick a box. "Shazam! It looks like you need some insulated socks, too." He snatched a pair and handed them to me.

While I slid them on, the boys started a WWE routine of some kind. The socks were navy blue and downright ugly. Then I put on the boots and tied them. In only a few seconds my feet were warm and cozy and dry. I walked around. They felt good. But the look? Yuck!

I went to the cash register and reached into my backpack, then I remembered that I didn't have any money. I sat back down and started taking the boots off. The boys stopped wrestling.

Nick said, "I thought you liked the boots."

"You know, not so much after all."

Nick looked at my old wet socks and leather boots. "Just keep those on. I'd feel really bad if your feet got frostbite and had to be amputated."

"But I don't have any—"

"Trav, can you put them on the squad's account? We are officially on an unofficial investigation regarding the haunting of Lay to Rest Cemetery and the case of Ivy's locket."

"Okey dokey, Smokey." He tossed my old boots and socks in a bag and gave it to me.

"Now," Nick said to me, "we can walk to the library."

"Say hello to your girlfriend for me," Travis said.

Girlfriend? Nick had a girlfriend?

chapter twenty-eight

THE LIBRARY

I STEPPED ONTO THE STREET, AND I HATED to admit it, but it felt nice to be in warm, dry shoes.

"Thanks," I said to Nick as we walked down the street to the library.

"You're welcome," Nick said. "Do you like them?"

"Yeah," I said. Maybe they weren't as bad as I originally thought.

"You could really use a heavier coat, hat, gloves, and scarf, too."

"I have some warmer stuff." My teeth chattered.

"We're here."

"This is the library?"

The plaque on the side of the building did, in fact, say BUTTERMILK RIVER COVE LIBRARY, but it was little more than a log cabin.

It was incredibly warm inside, heated by a pot-belly stove. There was a table in the center of the house, and except for the three windows, the walls were lined floor to ceiling with bookshelves. The farthest window looked at the hill. On the top was Lay to Rest. I hadn't noticed before, but with a white candle lit in each window, the Victorian looked nice.

Nick took off his puffy jacket. Under it he wore a navy henley tucked into jeans that were worn in all the right places. Nick caught me examining the faded back pockets, and a dimple appeared on his cheek. I looked at the floor.

Among a fortress of books was an old woman sitting at a desk. Nick approached her.

She jumped with a start when Nick said hi and put on glasses that magnified her eyes to the size of California navel oranges.

"Oh, Nicholas, is that you? How are you, dear?"

"I'm fine, Mrs. Schuldner."

"You look just like your daddy, you know that? I can remember him coming in here doing his home-work after school too. You look just like him, you know that?"

"Yes, ma'am."

"What's that?" She couldn't hear him.

More loudly Nick said, "Yes, ma'am, I know that I look like my father."

"Yes, you do. I remember when he used to come in after school and do his homework too."

I didn't have the heart to tell her it was a Saturday.

Nick kept his volume loud. "We're looking for local history."

"Doing your homework after school, just like your father. You look like a good student—are you? Do you work hard on your studies like your father?"

"Yes, ma'am. Where can we find information about people who used to live here, like a long time ago, like a list of people?"

"Lists? I don't think we have lists, but maybe old high school yearbooks would help." I didn't think yearbooks existed in 1825. "And then there are birth and death records, phone books, and I suppose the motor vehicle people would have lists of everyone who had a driver's license. Who are you looking for? Your father's old pal Lefty Short? He was a character, right handed and tall. Now, he wasn't a good student. He didn't do his homework after school the way your father did."

"No. It's not Lefty. It's someone who we think lived here a long time ago."

"Well, did he have a phone?"

"I don't know."

"For a good student, you don't know much. How about voting? You might be able to find voting records."

"I don't know."

"Do you even know who you're looking for, son?"

"Someone named Ivy," he said. "From 1825."

"1825! Holy Toledo! That was a long time ago." She grumbled, "1825." With a little grunt and a lot of effort, she stood up. She moved herself to a metal walker and used it to shuffle to a bookcase. A bony finger pointed to the spines of the books. "Can you read those?"

Nick said, "1800 to 1825, 1826 to 1850."

"Yes. That's them. Those are all the men who were registered to vote for those times. You could look through them to see if you find someone named Ivy. What a strange name. Did you ask your father? He might know. He's a very smart man. He got that way because he worked real hard in school. Do you work hard in school?"

"Yes, ma'am."

I spoke up for the first time. "What if Ivy is a woman?"

She looked toward my voice like she hadn't even realized there was another person in the room. She tried to focus her orange-size eyes on me. "Well, women didn't vote until 1920. So you'd have to start with the volume for 1920. You must not work hard at your studies or you'd know that."

I bowed my head like I'd just been punished.

Nick took the first volume off the shelf. "Thank you, Mrs. Schuldner."

I whispered to him, "Ask her about the tunnel."

She shouted at me, "Did you say TUNNELS?" Even though I'd whispered, she heard me. *Bizarre.*

"Yes, ma'am," I said.

"Oh my, well, let's see. There were some old mining tunnels, but that was a long time ago. The iron mines were closed up ages ago."

"Like when?" Nick asked.

"What's that?" she snapped, because now she was suddenly deaf again.

"WHEN?" Nick yelled to her.

"Before I was born, I suppose. That was 1932, and the mines were already closed up. The big business back in my day was railroads. Can you imagine, now we're going to the moon. Did you know that?"

"Yes, ma'am," Nick said.

"Of course you do. You're a good student. Like your father."

We sat side by side at the table and thumbed through the book. "Do *you* think Ivy could be a woman?" I asked.

"The locket kinda makes me think so."

"Me too," I said.

In a second Mrs. Schuldner was back in her chair, asleep.

"Sorry that my girlfriend was a little mean to you, but it's only because you don't work hard at your studies."

I punched him in the arm, and he pretended that it hurt. "She's your girlfriend?" I looked at her snoring. "I don't think I care if she doesn't like me."

We sat there scanning the voting log. There was no Ivy.

"I don't think this is going to help," I said.

"Me either. Let's come back when we have a better idea what we're looking for."

"Okay."

He quietly put the book back where we'd gotten it from, careful not to wake his girlfriend from her nap.

"Thanks for helping me with this," I said as we put on our coats and returned to the cold street.

"Sure," Nick said.

I said, "If you were a cop around here, you could investigate all the time. Probably be the sheriff one day and live in Buttermilk River Cove forever."

Maybe it was the way I said it that made him ask, "Would that be so bad? You know, you might like it here, if you gave it a chance."

"I have been giving it a chance."

"I can see that you're scared and hate creepy stuff, but you're *acting* a certain way so that we'll all like you," he said.

"What's wrong with wanting people to like me?"

"Nothing. I want people to like me, too. But did you ever think that maybe you don't have to act here?" Then he added, "Did you ever think that we'll like you the way you normally act?"

I hadn't considered this at all.

"Maybe you had to pretend in California, but you don't need to here."

"You really think that?"

"Well, there's one thing you need to do in order to fit in," Nick said.

"What?"

He looked at me thoughtfully. "Nah. Never mind. You wouldn't be able to handle it."

"Like heck." I pushed him at the shoulder, a little harder than I meant to, and he slipped on some ice and fell down. I put my hand over my mouth. "Nick, I'm sorry." I bent down and offered him my hand. "Are you okay?"

"I'm fine. My butt is wet, but I'm fine." He took my hand and tried to pull himself up. Instead, I slipped on the same patch of ice, and I fell on top of him.

"Ooof," he said, "Umm, could you . . ."

And I immediately got myself up and helped him up, for real this time.

"I'm sorry," I said again.

"It's okay. You know what? I don't care if you can't handle it. We're going. But first I need some dry pants."

"Where are we going to go?"

"To my house. I live right over here," he said. "That's where I keep my pants."

chapter twenty-nine

GOOG

A FEW FLURRIES FLOATED IN THE AIR AS WE headed to Nick's house.

Nick explained, "One of the great things about Buttermilk is that you can walk pretty much everywhere quickly because everything is close together."

We arrived at his house and went inside to find his mom taking down the Christmas tree.

"Hi, Ma," he said.

"Hello, dear." She put down her shoe box of red shimmery balls and came over to me. "And hello to you. I don't think I know you."

Nick said, "Ma, Sydney. Sydney, Ma." He was around the corner and down a hallway, but I heard him yell the intros. "I had an accident with some slush. I'm gonna put on some dry pants."

She shook my hand. "Are you from Dover?"

"No, Mrs. Wesley, I'm from California. My parents inherited Lay to Rest."

"Oh, that's nice," she said.

"Yeah," I awkwardly added. "It's nice."

Nick returned. "Ready?"

"I guess so."

Mrs. Wesley said, "She can't go like that." How did she know where I was going when I didn't?

"You're right." He looked at me, opened the hall closet, and took out a ski mask and pulled it over my head. Then he unzipped my coat and exchanged it for a purple ski jacket that was probably his mom's. He wrapped a scarf around my neck like ten times and finally slid my hands into Hulk-size gloves.

He and his mom tilted their heads to the side and examined me. "Better," he said.

Mrs. Wesley nodded. "Her legs will still be cold, so don't stay out long."

"I won't. I'm just going to bring her down the street then home."

"Okay. Then come right back," she said, and took a satiny red ball off the tree and put it into a shoe box. "Nice meeting you, Sydney."

"You too, Mrs. Wesley."

The coat was so puffy I had to pull my arms in to fit through the front door.

We approached the snowmobile.

"We're going on Goog?" I asked. But through the scarf and ski mask, Nick didn't hear me.

Nick got on. He put on a helmet and patted his hand on the seat behind him for me to sit. I did. Then he strapped a second helmet on my head over the ski mask. "Hold on."

"To what?" I asked, but he still didn't hear me.

He twisted the handles. As we zipped away, I wrapped my arms around his stomach. And off we went into the dusk. The chilled air made my eyes water. I had never been so grateful for an ugly ski mask.

Nick cruised around the main street, which was coated with just enough snow for Goog, pointing to things as we passed them, but I couldn't hear what he said.

We passed the library log cabin. All the lights were out. The police station was lit up. I saw only one uniformed guy inside. Nick pointed out houses and said things that I couldn't decipher in the wind.

He started up the hill. Its steepness caused me to slide off the back of Goog, so I had to hold on to Nick even tighter than I was already.

We were at the front of my house, and Nick drove Goog down the path into the graveyard. He stopped when we got to the farthest edge of the cemetery. He cut the engine. The town below looked like a Christmas-card village.

"It's a great view," he said. "So what did you think of that?"

"It was really cool. Thanks for taking me."

"You're welcome," he said. He looked around the graveyard. "This place is great."

"Yeah," I agreed. "Maybe it is."

"Do you mean that?"

"I really do," I said.

"How does it feel not to pretend that you like it?"

"Good." I smiled at Nick and at the sense of relief I felt over not having to act all the time.

He revved up Goog again, but I tapped him on the shoulder, signaling him to cut it off again.

"What's up?"

"About John Hancock—"

He interrupted, "I already know, but thanks for telling me." He turned the ignition back on and brought me to the front door. I took off the ski mask and gave it back.

"You can give me the coat later."

I nodded. "Seriously, Nick. Thanks for the ride, the boots, and taking me to the library."

"No problem, Mac." He took my helmet. "I think maybe you're starting to like Buttermilk River Cove."

"Yeah. I guess."

I watched Goog's headlights until I couldn't see them any longer.

We hadn't made any progress on the locket, but I had made progress on my relationship with this town.

chapter thirty

PROBLEM SOLVED?

AFTER I SHOWERED, I CLIMBED INTO BED with the locket. I'm not sure why, but I put it on and thought about Ivy.

Who was she?

Why was she haunting Lay to Rest?

Why was she haunting me? And why now?

I thought it had to do with the basement. She didn't want the renovations to hide her locket forever.

How could I figure all of this out?

I snapped up from bed.

Wait!

"The cemetery records!" I exclaimed to no one.

That's when it happened. . . .

Thud.

The first of the night.

"The records?" I asked Ivy.

Thud.

The thuds didn't scare me. Ivy heard me.

"Okay," I replied. "I will."

Thud.

chapter thirty-one

OATMEAL

I WOKE TO THE SOUND OF HAMMERING. JIM WAS on the roof—again.

I slippered down the stairs looking for Elliott. Instead, I found Roz in the kitchen. Her back was to me, and she was at the stove.

Uh-oh.

"Whatcha making, Roz?" I asked hesitantly.

She turned to me with a smile and held up a wooden spoon. "It's oatmeal. You want a taste?"

I was a little afraid, but then something registered in my brain that made my mouth water —it smelled good. I took a nibble. "Wow! How did you learn to do that?"

"I went to culinary school," Roz said proudly.

"You found a culinary school in Buttermilk River Cove?"

"Well, it wasn't exactly a school. Elliott hooked me up with a woman named Jackie O'Flynn who is the best cook around. She has a son in your class."

"Travis?"

"That's him! Elliott talked to her, and she invited me over. She taught me how to make oatmeal, egg salad, and grilled cheese sandwiches. We're having egg salad for lunch and grilled cheese sandwiches for dinner."

She dished out two bowls of oatmeal.

"You know what?" I asked.

"What, Sydney?"

"I don't remember the last time we had breakfast together."

She thought. "I guess it has been a long time."

I said, "If you ever told me that we would be sitting in the kitchen of a haunted Victorian house in the middle of a cemetery eating hot, delicious oatmeal, made by my mom, I wouldn't have believed you."

"Well, I'd agree with you, Syd, except about the haunted part. I thought we decided you were going to drop that."

"Correction. You decided that," I said.

"So, what are you doing today?"

"I was hoping Elliott could show me around the office. Would that be okay?"

"Of course it's okay. It's fantastic. I'm so glad you want to learn more about the business. You know, some day, this could all be yours." She looked out the back window at the gloomy sky and gray headstones.

This was a far cry from my dream to be a movie star. "Super," I said. My mom didn't pick up on the sarcasm; maybe there wasn't much there.

"Joyce has the day off, but Elliott is outside. I'm sure he'll show you whatever you want to learn," she said. "So do you like things a little better now? It sounded like you and your new friends had a good time the other night."

"Yeah. We did." I didn't tell her about the séance.

I stared out the window and savored my last buttery spoonful. "Do you think the sun will ever come out, Mom?"

She paused when I called her Mom but didn't say anything. "I sure hope so, Sydney."

It started to rain. Both the front and back doors flew open at the same time. My dad came in the front, Elliott in the back.

My dad said, "This rain will test my handiwork on the roof, huh?"

I glanced up, expecting water to start dripping from the ceiling, but it didn't.

"Do you want oatmeal?" Mom asked.

"Heck yeah!" Jim said. He dished some out for himself and Elliott.

Elliott took a taste and said, "This is wonderful. Did Joyce leave it?"

"Mom made it," I bragged.

"Really?" Jim paused. I wasn't sure if it was about the oatmeal, or that I'd called her Mom.

The wind whistled through the nooks and crannies of the old house. Elliott went to the workroom and returned with plain white pillar candles. He lit a few. "Just in case we lose the electricity," he said.

"Have you had electrical issues for a long time?" I asked. What I really wanted to know was *Have you been haunted before?* because according to Johanna hauntings and electrical snafus traveled together.

"Forever it seems. They come and go."

"What do you mean?"

"We'll have a few weeks when it all goes whacky. I'll get Joe Wesley from the hardware store up here to check things, and it's all fine. After a while, it goes away. It's fine for a long time and then happens again."

"Weird," I said, but I didn't think it was. I think Elliott had just described a continual series of hauntings. Either the spirits had found what they wanted and left, or they got tired of asking for help and not getting it. I wasn't going to let that happen to Ivy.

"Since I can't work outside, do you want to check out the attic?" my dad asked Mom. "I bet there's some cool stuff up there."

A big gust of wind blew again; the lights flickered and went out. *Out!*

Mom said, "Nope."

"Oh come on," Dad said. "Where's your sense of adventure? It'll be fun. I'll be right there with you the whole time. No ghosts are gonna get you." He squeezed her in a tight hug. "It might even be a little romantic. Besides, what else are you going to do on an ugly day like this?"

Dad pulled her out of the room.

"I guess I'm going to the attic. Sydney, maybe Elliott can show you that stuff in the office now. Oh, and send a rescue squad if I'm not back to make egg salad."

They retired to the attic, each double-fisted with candles. I didn't imagine my mom was going to last long up there.

chapter thirty-two

THE MAP

"WHAT DO YOU WANT TO DO IN THE OFFICE?" Elliott asked.

"Can you show me how we keep records of the . . . the . . . souls?"

He lit the last candle. "Sure . . . ," he said hesitantly. "Do you want to tell me why you are suddenly interested in the souls?"

"Can't a girl change her mind?"

"Sure a girl can. But I don't think you have. What's up?" he asked.

"Seriously? You wanna know?"

He nodded.

"Promise you won't laugh?"

He made an X over his heart.

I filled him in on the thuds, the séance, the tunnel,

the oven, the brick, and the locket. He listened to the whole thing and didn't laugh once. It felt good to get it out and tell someone the truth, that at first I had just wanted her to leave and not possess anyone, but now I wanted to help her.

"Let me see it," he said.

I unhooked the locket from my neck. "I thought that if I could find Ivy in the Lay to Rest records, I could figure out who she was, and maybe what she wants me to do with the locket."

"Well, that sounds like a good plan. But we'll have a lot to comb through with only the name Ivy. We have decades of records."

"The brick said 1825. So we only have to look at one year."

The excitement faded from his face. "Bad news, Syd. There was a big fire, around the turn of the century. All the records earlier than 1900 were destroyed."

Ugh. "I'll have to think of something else. I guess I could check out every stinking tombstone in the place."

"Checking every headstone would work, but it would take a very long time." He dropped his chin onto his fist like he was thinking hard. Then he snapped his head up. "I have an idea." He took a candle and disappeared, leaving me all alone at the table with the wind punching against the house. A few days ago I would've been scared enough to pee myself, but I sat by candlelight without even a flinch.

Elliott reappeared in the room. If I'd just met his pale face with its extra dabs of eyeliner and lipstick, his neck wrapped in a snug scarf like Freddy from *Scooby-Doo*, I'd run in fear. But he smiled, and his eyes filled with kindness and enthusiasm when he held up a giant scroll, like an architect's plans. "This," he said, "just might help."

He rolled a rubber band off one end and unrolled a huge grid. "This is all computerized now, but we can look at how Lay to Rest is organized and decipher where people were buried in 1825. That will narrow down the search." He pointed to the plot in the first row, first column. "This is the first person buried in 1602. And as you move to the right you see the next several. For the first hundred and fifty years this was a family cemetery." Then he pointed to an area with small words and dates. "In 1749 she officially opened for business. The graves are marked here with the last name and date of death."

I studied the paper. All the deaths were April through November. "Isn't it weird that no one died in the winter?"

"They did, but they weren't buried because the ground was too frozen to dig."

"So they were . . . were . . ."

"Cremated."

"Lovely," I said.

"It's a fact of the business, Syd," Elliott said.

"I know. I get it. That doesn't mean I like it." I looked at the grid some more. "What's this?" I pointed to a small area way off to the side of the cemetery.

"That's called a potter's field. It's a space where people without money to pay for a plot are buried. There are no headstones and no records of those people."

"So, if Ivy is a first name, this map won't show her. If she died in the winter, this map won't show her. And if she was too poor to afford a plot, this won't show her."

"Right, but it will show us the section of the cemetery in which people were buried in 1825. And that's right here." He pointed a manicured finger to the spots dated 1825. "If she died in Buttermilk

River Cove in the spring, and could afford a burial, we can look for her in that section."

It was our only lead. "What's this?" I pointed to a square on the paper.

"That's a mausoleum. They don't really follow the date pattern. They have spaces for generations of family members to be included."

"So if she's in a mausoleum, we probably won't find her."

"Only by going inside each one and looking at the plaques," he said.

"Fab! That sounds like hours of great fun."

chapter thirty-three

THE MESSAGE

I WORE THE LOCKET TO SCHOOL THE NEXT day. I went to Johanna's and Mel's cubbies. "My idiot brother can bring us," Johanna said. "He's going anyway."

"Cool," Mel said.

"Wanna go, Mac?" Johanna asked.

"Sure," I said. *Yay!* "Where?"

"The hockey game tonight. Our Bulldogs are playing the Hyenas. They'll probably have glow sticks. I love glow sticks"

"I don't think I've ever had a glow stick. But I love the idea of them," I said.

Mel said, "Then you're in for a real treat." But I could tell she didn't think glow sticks were a treat at all.

"Hey." Johanna eyed the locket. "Can I wear it for a while?"

My hand immediately went to my neck.

Johanna said, "I thought that since I was such a spiritual Magoo the other night"—I caught a glimpse of Mel rolling her eyes at Johanna's use of Magoo—"Ivy might try to communicate with me through the locket. You know, since I have a gift and all."

I thought she totally made sense. "Be careful with it."

"You betcha, Macky Magoo." She went to class sliding the locket around her neck with her thumb and index finger.

I was the first one at the lunch table. I sat all alone for a few minutes, but anyone who has ever sat alone at a lunch table knows that sitting alone feels like forever. I pretended to be very busy in my backpack looking for something important, very important.

Ah, I found it.

A pen!

By then Travis had joined me.

He unpacked a tuna salad on a hamburger roll and a bag of ranch-flavored chips, lifted off the bun, laid the chips on top of the tuna, put the top of the bun back on, and pushed till the chips crunched. "Did ya hear?"

"Hear what?" I asked.

"Ivy gave JoJo a message." He took a big, crunchy bite. "It's in code."

Nick sat next to me. "Did ya hear?"

"Yeah. What's the code? What does it mean?" I asked.

"It was some random numbers. Johanna thinks it's a combination to a lock," Nick said. He unpacked his lunch: meat loaf sandwich, apple, pretzels, and container of cafeteria-bought chocolate milk.

"Well, where is she?" I asked. "I have to see it."

Travis set down the last few bites of his sandwich and rested his fingers on his temples. He closed his eyes.

"What are you doing?" Nick asked.

"I'm summoning Johanna to come to the cafeteria and tell us about the code."

Mel walked in with Johanna on her heels. "Check it out," Travis said. "She can read my mind."

"Amazing," I said.

Johanna and Mel sat. Our eyes were glued to Johanna.

"What are you guys staring at?" Mel asked.

"I called you with my mind," Travis said. "And then you appeared."

"I did? My mind was telling me to go to the caf. Do you think I'm telephonic? It's like I have mental Wi-Fi."

"Telepathic," Nick corrected. "Or it was lunchtime, so you came to the place where we eat lunch."

"Watch this," Johanna said. "I bet I can guess what's in my lunchbox without looking."

"So can I," Nick said. "Chicken spread on an English muffin."

She frowned at him. "I can't be expected to crack this code when I'm around such negativity."

"What's the code?" I asked. She handed me a little paper, folded up really tight. "Where did this come from?"

"I was fiddling with the locket and it opened. This was inside."

I unfolded it.

"It's a mystery," she said as I read the paper. Johanna continued, "I'm sure I can solve it—"

"I already have," I said. They looked at me with surprise. "I know exactly where Ivy wants us to go. At least, I know where this paper is telling us to go. Meet me at my house. Six o'clock. Wear your sludgekickers. It's gonna be muddy in the graveyard."

chapter thirty-four

36-14H

IT WAS VERY MUDDY. AND COLD. AND THEN it started snowing. "The paper had numbers and a letter: 36-14H," I told my friends as we went into the cemetery. "They're coordinates to a specific location in this grave-yard." My feet were totally dry in the sludge-kickers Nick had gotten me. "Thirty-six is a row." We approached the front tombstones. "This is row one, row two, row three." I walked and counted until I got to thirty-six.

"Now what?" Travis asked.

I said, "Fourteen is the headstone number. We want the fourteenth from the edge."

We followed the tombstones down the row and counted. But there were only thirteen. The next thing in the row was something we all knew well: the Dolan mausoleum.

Johanna said, "I just got déjà voodoo."

"Why would Ivy have a paper with the location number of this place?" Travis asked.

Nick took the paper from me. "How would Ivy know the cemetery's numbering system?"

I shrugged, because I had no idea. Bravely I said, "We have to find crypt H."

Mel said, "What are you waiting for?"

I leaned into the heavy door. Its bottom scraped on the cement floor. Mel nudged me forward. "Go on," she said, and she aimed the flashlight in front of me.

The walls were lined with rectangular slabs of stone, each with a small metal plaque on which there was a name, birth date, and death date. The first was BEATRICE DOLAN, APRIL 16, 1712–AUGUST 30, 1763. My friends were close behind me, also studying words in the flashlight's beam. I shined it from one plaque to the next until I got to the one that must've been H.

IVY SHAW
MARCH 16, 1849–APRIL 13, 1862

"We found her," I said.

We all stood there for a minute and stared, not sure

what to do. Ivy was on the other side of this stone.

Why did she want me to come here?

Nick said, "She was our age when she died."

"So I guess that does it," Travis said. "We found her. Mystery solved. Now she can rest easy, or cross over, or run into the light, or whatever it is people do when they're done haunting. Adios. See ya later, alligator. Now can we go get some cocoa?"

"That's too easy," I said.

"I like easy," Travis said. "Rhymes with squeezy and cheesy."

"Open it," Mel said.

"Are you crazy?" Travis asked. "Let's just go to the hockey game and say adios to this muchacha."

Mel said, "No game for us. We're too close."

"Totally," Johanna agreed, "but I have to say, opening someone's grave is a great way to *get* haunted, not a way to get *un*haunted."

Mel said, "You just wanna leave and go to watch a hockey game instead and let poor Syd be haunted forever?"

"No, we're not just gonna leave," Johanna said. She took Mel's hand and Travis's. "I was going to suggest that we say a few words and send her on her way."

Nick took my hand.

Johanna started. "We are gathered here today to bid farewell to Ivy. Hopefully, she can rest in peace now," she said. "Now everyone say a few words."

Travis said, "You were a cool ghost."

Johanna tugged at his arm.

Mel said, "You added a little excitement to this place. Thanks."

Nick said, "Good-bye, Ivy."

I was thinking of what to say. The only thing on my mind was *Nick is holding my hand! Nick is holding my hand!* "I guess I'm kinda psyched to sleep through the night, but I'll miss you a little too."

Johanna said, "Good. Okay. Now we can go."

We let go of hands and went to the door.

On the way to the Victorian, Mel said, "Well, that was kind of a letdown. I expected something more dramatic or gruesome or something."

"Cocoa will make you feel better." Travis put a comforting arm over her shoulder. "It always works for me."

Inside was warm and cozy. Joyce ladled out cocoa for everyone, including One and Two in their pajamas.

"Hey! Hey!" Travis said to them.

"Trav-dawg," One said.

"Sweet T," Two said.

Nick asked them, "How's the cocoa?"

"Great!" they said.

"See you later, percolator," One said, and the twins left.

"Are they your new friends?" I asked Travis and Nick.

"Sure. We go the same school," Nick said.

Travis added, "They remind me of me. Of course, it takes two of them to equal one of me."

Then Joyce excused herself for the night. I sat at the table surrounded by my four new friends. They liked my house, my cemetery, my clothes; they didn't even mind my brothers. I felt totally comfortable just sitting here, not acting or pretending anything. It should've felt great, but I felt . . . empty.

"What's wrong, Mac?" Johanna asked.

I said, "I can't believe she's gone. I think I expected to meet her or something."

Travis said, "That would've been tough, considering she's dead."

The lights blinked. Suddenly the room became very cold. I reached down and grabbed Nick's hand under the table. He squeezed mine.

"We're not done," Johanna said. "She wants us to do something else."

"What?" I asked.

"She didn't say," Johanna said.

"She's talking to you?" Travis asked.

"She's talking to all of us right now," Johanna said.

The lights blinked some more.

I could see my breath in the air, and my nose felt like it was struck with ice.

"Weird," Travis said.

"Cool," Mel said.

One by one the lights returned to normal.

"What now?" I asked. "We need to think."

"Maybe Mrs. Dolan knows something," Nick said. "After all, Ivy was buried in her family's mausoleum."

"Then we'll have to ask her," I said.

The room fell silent like I'd said something very, very wrong.

"What?" I asked. "We can ask her, can't we?"

"She doesn't leave her house," Johanna said.

"Which is big and old and scary and filled with cats," Nick said.

"Maybe she'll let us in," I said.

"I like the way you think, Mac," Mel said.

"We're going to her cursed old house that's filled with cats, aren't we?" Travis asked.

chapter thirty-five

MRS. DOLAN AND FRANNY BUTTERS

THE NEXT DAY WE STOOD ON MRS. DOLAN'S front porch, which was as far on the edge of town as you could get. Buttermilk River Cove houses were small and close together, except the Victorian and Mrs. Dolan's.

It was a massive brick old-fashioned Colonial house. On one side there was a two-story tower that came to a peak. The windows of the tower were dark. In fact, all but one window was dark against the late afternoon gray sky. Through that window I could see a fire was lit, and someone sat in a rocking chair.

"Is that her?" I asked.

Nick said, "I've never seen her before."

"She doesn't look scary," I said, but then I jumped

because something brushed against my leg. It was a cat.

We approached the door. There was a brass knocker the size of my fist.

"Go on," Mel said.

I lifted and dropped it. It made a heavy *klunk*! Almost instantly I heard locks twisting on the other side of the door, lock after lock after lock.

Finally, the door opened, revealing a tall, thin woman looking a bit younger than my grandmother. She wore a long skirt and a yellow button-up sweater.

She smiled when she saw us. "Hello, children."

"Mrs. Dolan?" I asked. "My name is Sydney Mackenzie. I'm new to town. I live at Lay to Rest."

"Of course. I know who you are. You're Teddy's great-niece. You can't keep anything quiet around these parts. Please come in, come in. The kitties love company, and they don't get much, I'm afraid."

We walked into a great entryway that was dimly lit by a giant crystal chandelier. To the left there was a darkened room where all the furniture was covered with white sheets. To the right was a welcoming living room with a burning fire.

"Please leave your shoes by the door. I like to keep things tidy."

We lined up our muddy boots by the front door and followed her into the living room. It was cozy and warm, with cats curled up in little beds wherever one could be tucked.

"Look, babies, we have company." A few furry heads turned to look at us; most yawned and lay back down. A few came over to sniff. "Please, sit."

Travis, Mel, and Johanna sat on a high-backed, fancy-looking couch. Nick and I each sat in a chair on either side of the couch. Mrs. Dolan sat back in her rocking chair. I noticed a basket of knitting at one foot and a small metal tank at her other foot. A cat jumped into her lap, and she petted it.

A cat jumped into Travis's lap, then Johanna's, then Mel's. Soon a very puffy white cat hopped onto Nick, and a calico about the size of a bear nudged himself onto my lap. All of the cats were petted.

"So what brings you to our home?" she asked.

"I was wondering if you knew someone," I said.

"Oh, I know lots of people. Sadly, many of my friends and family have passed on."

"I guess that's what happens when you get old," Travis said.

We all looked at him like he had the worst manners in the world. He tried again. "What I meant to say was, that's good, because this person we're wondering about is dead too." We looked at him like this was still rude. He pretended to take a key and lock his mouth closed.

"Do you know something about someone named Ivy Shaw?"

"Ivy?" she asked.

"Yes, ma'am," I said. "It would've been a long time ago. She died in—"

"1825," she said.

"How did you know that?"

"I have a very good memory. I can remember all kinds of dates and names."

"What can you tell us about her?" Nick asked.

"Do you mind if I ask you why you want to know?"

"Well, it's silly actually. You probably wouldn't be interested." I figured she would think that the idea of Ivy haunting me would be crazy.

"I've heard lots of silly things. Why don't you try me?" She reached down to the tank at her feet and picked up a clear plastic face mask. She held it to her mouth and nose and inhaled deeply.

Nick sorta nodded at me, so I told her about the thuds in the night, the Ouija board, the tunnel, the locket, the paper message, and her family mausoleum. She nodded and uh-huhed a lot.

"So that's why we're here. To see if you can help us figure out what Ivy wants us to do," I said.

"I'm glad you told me that story," she said. "Now I'll tell you one that might be helpful." She looked at the picture over the fireplace. "That is a picture of my great-great-grandmother, Frances Marie Dolan. She and her family owned all the land in this cove. Back then it was a milk farm—a buttermilk farm to be specific—and a cemetery." She looked at me. "Our relatives have been friends for generations. My family did very well selling their milk all around Delaware, Maryland, and parts of Virginia. As you can imagine, it was a very big job for a small family. So Franny Butters, as she was known at the time, bought slaves. They lived in the main house, right here where we're sitting, and ran the farm. She taught them to read and write and slowly tried to bring more of their families to the cove."

We listened without making a sound.

"She also dabbled in potions, which was not popular. Because of that, people said she was cursed."

"I heard you were cursed," Travis said.

We looked at him with gaping mouths. He relocked his lips.

"It's okay," Mrs. Dolan said. "Rumors like that tend to linger."

"What happened?" Nick asked.

"The slaves died. One by one they all died young. People said it was because of Franny Butters's curse. She couldn't run the farm without their help, so she slowly started selling off pieces of the land and the cattle." Then she added, "Besides, when word of the curse spread, people didn't want to buy her milk."

Nick said, "What does this have to do with Ivy?"

"Ivy was one of the slaves. According to the story, she was the last to die. And that was right before emancipation in—"

"1863," Nick said. We looked at him, surprised. "I'm good with dates too."

"How did they die?" I asked.

Mrs. Dolan didn't answer. Instead, she inhaled another deep breath of oxygen and gently scooted the cat off her lap, stood, and straightened her skirt. "Follow me. I think you can learn more on your own."

chapter thirty-six

THE STUDY

MRS. DOLAN CROSSED THE GRAND ENTRY-way and slowly walked into the dark room where the furniture was covered with sheets. She stopped at a shelf and picked up a four-pronged candelabra. She struck an extra-long match and lit all four candles. "The electricity and heat are off on this side of the house. Since it's just me and the cats, I keep this wing shut down."

"Where are we going?" Travis asked.

"To the study. Franny Butters kept meticulous journals."

We walked down a windowless hallway and up a spiral staircase. Mrs. Dolan breathed deeply and heavily. She set her candelabra down on a massive wooden desk. Then she took hold of a ladder that was attached to floor-to-ceiling bookshelves and slid it to a section of books that looked the most worn of the collection.

"The shelves here are dated 1825, so that's where you'll find information about Ivy. If you don't mind, I must excuse myself for a moment. It's five o'clock, and I feed the kitties promptly at five every night. It won't take me long, and I'll come back to see how you're doing. You're welcome to read anything you like. And don't rush." She walked away very slowly. I could hear her breathing even after I couldn't see her.

Nick climbed up the ladder and scanned the bindings.

"How freakin' cool is this place?" Mel asked.

"Do you see anything about the potions, Nick?" Johanna asked.

"Actually, I do," Nick said. He carefully slid a volume off the shelf. "This one says 'Potions 1825.'" He passed it down to Johanna, who cracked it open and sunk deep into an enormous dark brown leather chair.

Nick continued looking at the books. "Here is something you might be interested in, Mac."

"What?"

"It says 'Notes by Ivy Shaw, 1862.'"

I eagerly took it. I sat at the desk in an oversize chair that could easily accommodate two people. And it did, because Nick fell into the seat next to me.

Ivy's writing was messy. It reminded me of the twins'. Her entries were short.

> *Practiced reading with Miss Franny Butters*
> *Learning about bugs*
> *Alphonso left today*
> *Went to town today*
> *Sold a lot of buttermilk today*
> *Helped Miss Franny Butters with a potion today*
> *Jeremiah left today*
> *Dug a grave today. Mr. Mackenzie paid me 50 cents*
> *Mary left today*
> *Worked at the graves today*
> *I am leaving tomorrow*

"She helped at the cemetery, too," Nick said. "That's how she knew the numbering system."

I said, "She says people left, not died."

"Maybe she just didn't use the word 'die.' You know, like when people say they 'went to a better place,'" Johanna suggested, her nose still in the potion book.

"Maybe. But she said she's leaving tomorrow. She wouldn't know she was going to a better place tomorrow," Mel added.

"It looks like she died before she could leave the farm," I said. "It's a shame that she never got to be free. Just one more year, and she would've been emancipated."

I asked Johanna, "What do you have in the potion book?"

"Some of the usual. Stuff for a cold, fever, sore throat, headache, swollen ankles, colicky baby, chicken pox. Looks like she experimented with a love potion, but it never worked," Johanna said. "Actually, it looks like most of these didn't work. Good thing she was good at buttermilk, because it doesn't look like she was a good potioner . . . potionist."

Mel read over Johanna's shoulder and pointed to a page. "There was one that she was good at—the Potion of the Two-Day Sleep."

"That's funny," Nick said.

"Funny?" Travis asked. "How? I don't get it."

"Not funny *ha-ha,* funny *strange,* because it reminds me of the John Hancock story Mac told us. Remember?"

How could I forget?

"Right," I said.

"How could anyone forget that." Nick gave me a knowing look. I'd have to tell my friends that I'd made that up.

I read Ivy's last entry out loud to everyone:

I will hide the truth.

A wind came out of nowhere and blew out our candles. We had only the tiny bit of light coming through the skylights. The temperature dropped. I knew Ivy well enough by now to know that she was telling me something. "There's something important about that entry," I said.

"She hid something," Johanna said.

"She wants us to find it," Mel said.

"I wonder where it is," Nick said.

I said, "She already told us."

chapter thirty-seven

THE CRYPT

AND THAT'S HOW WE ENDED UP AT THE
Dolan mausoleum.

Again.

This time Nick brought a crowbar from Cork's
stash of tools. The wind whipped between the tombstones, only a sliver of moon shone from behind
dark clouds in a black sky. My hands were numb
with cold.

"We're going in there again? Why?" Travis asked.

"We're not just going in," I said.

"We're opening Ivy's crypt." Nick finished my
sentence for the others.

"No freakin' way," Travis said.

Mel said, "Now you're talking."

Pushing the heavy door open this time wasn't

nearly as scary as the last two times. It made me feel like maybe I was getting used to Creepsville.

We stood in front of Ivy's crypt. "Ready, Nick?"

"Ready."

I looked at the ceiling. "Ivy, I hope this is what you wanted us to do." I handed Johanna the flashlight. "Shine it right here." I pointed to the crack in the stone under the plaque.

Nick wedged the crowbar in the same spot and pushed. It didn't budge. "How about a little help, Trav?"

Travis leaned into the crowbar with Nick, but still no movement. So Mel joined them and then the stone plate popped off.

There was an envelope. I recognized the handwriting—it matched that in the book we'd seen at Mrs. Dolan's house.

It was Ivy's.

* chapter thirty-eight *
THE LETTER

THE LETTER IN THE ENVELOPE SAID:

Today is April 13, 1862.

I will die today and begin a new life as a free person.

I want to leave a message so people will know the truth.

Mrs. Dolan gives me the Potion of the Two-Day Sleep and tells everyone I am dead.

They believe she is cursed because another slave died. I am the last one.

I will crawl through the secret tunnel to the woods. Mr. Mackenzie picks me up on a horse and brings me to New York to be with my family.

I will be free in New York.

"That's what she wanted us to know," I said.

"The Dolans were never cursed," Johanna said. "They just let everyone believe that."

"They're heroes," Nick said. "But they had to keep it a secret."

"Yeah, secret heroes," Travis agreed.

"And the secret was almost buried in my basement forever."

"That's so cool," Mel said. "Something exciting and wonderful did happen in Buttermilk River Cove. It was a big part of the Underground Railroad."

"And my family helped," I said in awe.

chapter thirty-nine

FIRST CUSTOMER

WE KNEW THE TRUTH, AND I STILL COULDN'T sleep.

There had to be more.

The story couldn't end there.

So I got up and did something I'd avoided for days. I sat in my bed and did my time capsule project. I wrote an essay all about a woman named Franny Butters and a man named Ted Mackenzie. How they created a scheme involving a potion, an oven, and a tunnel to secretly move slaves to freedom. Since no one could know the truth, Franny Butters let everyone believe she was cursed. She had no one to work on her farm, so she had to sell large sections of her land, on which everyone in Buttermilk River Cove now lived. I added a page about a young girl named Ivy, explained what I imagined her escape was like and how she returned from the grave to make sure the story was told, and how I was proud to be the one to help her tell it.

I reread the essay. It was good. It read like it could be a screenplay . . . starring Emiline Hunt. Or better, *me!*

When I went downstairs for breakfast the next morning, the table was filled with people—Cork, Elliott, and my parents—Joyce was stirring a pot of what smelled like an encore performance of Mom's oatmeal.

"What's going on? Why is everyone up so early?"

"We have our first customer," my dad said.

"Oh," I said. "That's sad and good at the same time."

Joyce said to my mom and dad, "I've contacted her children, and they're on their way. They want to have the service tomorrow."

"We can do that," Cork said. "On account that we don't have to dig through the frozen ground. I can get the mausoleum ready today."

"I'll begin on the flowers," Elliott said. "She may not have been a popular woman in this town, but that doesn't mean I can't make things pretty for her. It will be lovely."

"Wait. Not popular?" I asked. "Are you talking about Mrs. Dolan? Did she die?"

"Yes," Mom answered. "Did you know her?"

By the time I got to school, the kids already knew about Mrs. Dolan.

It was time to bury the time capsule. The whole school gathered in the gym around a big metal box. One at a time, everyone said what they had done and then dropped their contribution into the steel case.

The little kids started. One and Two went up together and dropped in a picture they had drawn of Booger Boy, a superhero they'd invented who constantly had a cold and used his cape as a tissue.

Travis was the first eighth grader to go. He held up our yearbook from last year. "In twenty-five years we can look back at this and remember what we looked like when we were in middle school."

Then it was my turn.

I held up a pink composition notebook. "This is a story I wrote about something I recently learned. It's about my ancestors and some special stuff that happened here in Buttermilk River Cove. I want to make sure the story isn't forgotten. This way someone will read about it again in twenty-five years."

"That's very nice, Sydney," Principal Perkel said. "Maybe you can tell us the story."

"I think it would be good for everyone to hear," I said. I tossed the notebook in. It landed with a *thud*.

For the next twenty-four hours the cemetery buzzed with preparations. Elliott drove into the city and picked up spring-colored flowers to decorate the mausoleum. I helped him sweep out the inside of the stone house. We laid a white runner on the ground, and Elliott placed small votive candles a few feet apart along the edges of the walls. Between them he placed bunches of yellow and white flowers. "They look like buttermilk," he said.

Soon enough, a small line of cars paraded from the church up the hill to Lay to Rest. I counted them. Only five cars of people to send this woman to her eternal slumber. I guessed that was the price you paid for letting people believe you were cursed.

People gathered outside the Dolan mausoleum. There were tears and hugging and shivering in the cold. They broke their sadness only to comment on the decor.

Then a shocking thing happened. The clouds

drifted away from the sun, and warm light shone on the cemetery. I held my face up to it.

I've missed you.

The temperature must've risen ten degrees, bringing it above freezing for the first time since my arrival here. The minister said it was Mrs. Dolan shining down from heaven. I hung around and listened to the short service.

A few of the guests lingered on the Victorian's wraparound porch.

A woman approached me and wrapped me in a cuddly hug. "Sydney," she said, setting me free, "your family has been so good to us through all of this. The cemetery and the house look great. You've really brightened things up."

I turned to look at the Victorian. She was right. I hadn't noticed all the work my parents, Elliott, Cork, and Joyce had done. The roof was straight and new, the porch swing was hung, the front door was painted, the fence was replaced, the windows were cleaned, and the creeping vines were trimmed back. Elliott had twined white lights around the porch railing and the holly trees in the yard.

I looked back at the woman and wondered how she knew my name, then I remembered that it was a small town and everybody knew everybody.

"I wanted to come introduce myself—I'm Mrs. Dolan's daughter," she said. "My name is Frannie."

"Like Franny Butters?"

"Exactly like Franny Butters, except I use an *i-e* at the end. I was named after her. When I was a little girl," she said, "I used to think a hunchback who ate bugs lived up there." She pointed to the attic that my mom was trying to make into a bright, cheery den and laughed at herself.

I laughed too, because the hunchback legend had made it all the way to my new friends.

Her laughter attracted the attention of another woman, who looked to be in her midtwenties and African American.

Frannie gave her a big hug. "And this is my cousin, Marie."

"We're not *actually* related," Marie said. "Did you know her?"

"I just met her for the first time the other day. She helped me and my friends with some local history research we were doing."

"Oh yeah?" the woman asked. "I love history. What was the project?"

The minister came over and interrupted. "It's so

good to see you." He hugged young Frannie. "You don't come home often enough." Then he hugged the other woman. "Marie! My dear Marie Shaw-Lane! Aren't you a sight for sore eyes! I'm so glad to see you."

Marie SHAW?

chapter forty

MARIE SHAW

"MARIE SHAW?" I SQUAWKED A LITTLE too loudly, because Marie looked around self-consciously, like I'd embarrassed her. "Sorry," I said.

"Yes," she said in a calming way. "I was named after Franny Butters also. Her middle name was Marie."

"I know, but your last name . . . Is your ancestor Ivy Shaw?"

She looked stunned. "She is. That's why we've always kept Shaw as part of our last name, every generation. How did you know that?"

"It's a long story," I said.

"I'd really like to hear it," Marie said.

"Do you like hot cocoa?"

* * *

We went inside the Victorian and sat at the table with our cocoa.

"Do you believe in ghosts?" I asked.

Her eyes got big like I'd said something crazy. I was ready to say, *Ha-ha! Just kidding!* when she looked at me, dead serious, and said, "Yes." Then Marie said, "I always feel like there are spirits around me."

I said, "I want to tell you something really weird."

"Okay," Marie said.

"Ever since I moved here, Ivy Shaw has been haunting me."

She stared at me. "Haunting?"

"Well, maybe not haunting. It was more like visiting."

"Sounds like a haunting," she said.

I told her about the séance, the tunnel, and the brick. "That's where I found this." I pulled the locket out from under my shirt. "I think she wanted me to find it because inside were directions to a hidden letter."

Marie carefully took the locket from me and studied the charm. "Did you find the letter?"

"Yes." I didn't tell her that we'd broken into her family crypt. "I think she wanted someone to know the story of what happened here."

I told her that Franny Butters had mastered only one potion, the Potion of the Two-Day Sleep. "She wanted to help free slaves. So she partnered with my relatives who owned this cemetery. Their scheme was a good one. Franny would give the slaves the potion, making it look like they were dead. Then they woke up and crawled through the tunnel to the woods, where someone took them to New York, where they could be free."

"I've heard pieces of that story before, but not the whole thing. Now I know why I was named after her," Marie said. "She was a wonderful woman."

"She made a big sacrifice," I said. "Ivy came to me so that I would know her story."

Marie thought for a minute. "Don't you think more people should know this story?"

"I totally do."

Marie grinned. "Did I tell you what I do for a living?"

IVY'S LOCKET—
THE MOVIE

IT TURNED OUT THAT MARIE LIVED IN NEW York City, where she was a film writer. She wrote and sold the screenplay for *Ivy's Locket.*

Guess where the movie was filmed?

Joyce and her hot cocoa were especially popular. Dad, Cork, and Nick's uncle Joe helped with the props, and Mom and Mrs. O'Flynn made oatmeal and egg salad everyday. Even Nick's girlfriend, old Mrs. Schuldner, consulted on local history. She was treated like a queen in her very own director's chair and outfitted with headphones the size of earmuffs.

IVY'S LOCKET—SCENE 21:
CEMETERY SCENE

CAST

SYDNEY MACKENZIE .... Emiline Hunt

GHOST OF IVY SHAW .... Sydney Mackenzie

SUPPORTING GHOST 1 .... Nick Wesley

SUPPORTING GHOST 2 .... Travis O'Flynn

SUPPORTING GHOST 3 .... Johanna Stevens

SUPPORTING GHOST 4 .... Melanie Healey

BRENDAN MACKENZIE .... Brendan Mackenzie

AIDAN MACKENZIE .... Aidan Mackenzie

SYDNEY MACKENZIE runs through Lay to Rest
Cemetery.

THE GHOST OF IVY SHAW chases her.

SUPPORTING GHOSTS sit on tombstones.

SYDNEY MACKENZIE falls and lets out a blood
curdling scream as THE GHOST OF IVY SHAW
descends upon her.

GHOST OF IVY SHAW
Pleeeeasse, you must find my locket and give it to
my great-great-great-granddaughter!

SYDNEY
[Shakes in fear]
O-o-kay . . . I'll help you.

And make sure the world knows what happened
here in Buttermilk River Cove.

SYDNEY
I . . . I p-p-p-promise . . . or . . .
or I'll kiss a cow's butt.

GHOST OF IVY SHAW flies away.

The director, a Hollywood legend known only as
Santoro, yelled through a megaphone, "Cut! That's
a wrap. Good job, everyone. I think we have a hit on
our hands."

Everyone on the film crew clapped.

It was going to be a great film, even though Hollywood had taken a few liberties with the truth. My
friends and I high-tenned as the crew began packing
up the set. Santoro patted Elliott on the back to
thank him for his work with the makeup.

Emiline Hunt stood on a costume trunk and took
the megaphone. "Before you all go," she yelled, "I'd
like to make an announcement."

Reporters and photographers who had been limited

to my front yard during the filming were allowed back to hear her.

Flashbulbs ignited, and microphones were put under our mouths for comments.

We posed for a few shots that I hoped would show up in *Teen People* or *Us Weekly*.

Mrs. Dolan's cats ran, pranced, and played around us and all through the tombstones. Turns out those formerly fat, lazy cats loved to run around outside, and they loved living with me. Johanna, Nick, and Mel each took one too. Travis and Mrs. Schuldner each took two.

Emiline cleared her throat. "On behalf of Logan Pictures, Bergen Entertainment Group, and myself, we would like to thank the people of Buttermilk River Cove for their hospitality during the making of this film, especially the Mackenzie family for the use of their amazing cemetery."

She continued, "Mayor Margreither, as a token of our appreciation, we're pleased to present a grant to the town of Buttermilk River Cove for renovations of your school buildings, the creation of a drama department, and the creation of a community center. And we would like to treat the cast and crew to dinner at the Pizza Palace!"

Everyone clapped and roared about the generous

donations to the town. More photos were taken and interviews continued.

A short while later, ghostly makeup washed off, Nick and I went to the Pizza Palace, where we met my parents, the gang from the cemetery, Emiline Hunt, the film crew, and all my friends from Buttermilk River Cove.

Nick held open the Pizza Palace door for me. "Our usual booth?" he asked.

"Nah," I said. "Let's try a table today."

As we were eating, my new cell phone vibrated. It was a text from Leigh.

Leigh: Everyone is watching U on the Entertainment channel. U did it! Come back now!

Me: No way.

Leigh: Why? What's going on there?

Me: I'm having pizza with my new friends.

Leigh: Sounds boring!

Me: Nope. They're great friends. Actually, it's a perfect day in Buttermilk River Cove, and I don't want to leave.

I reached deep into the back pocket of my jeans and pulled out a card to show Nick.

"You did it!" he said. "Your next slice is free!"

LIKE DELAWARE, LITTLE BUT IMPORTANT

YOU MIGHT BE WONDERING HOW MUCH OF this story is true.

Well, I can assure you that it's all fiction. Okay, so, it's *mostly* fiction: There are probably five friends who think one of them is being haunted. They could've built a time capsule. There really is a state called Delaware in which there is surely an old lady with a big house filled with cats, people with secrets, and cemeteries. Some people in Delaware believe that there are haunted places.

What is *not* fiction is that there were slaves in Delaware, and the state was a very important stop on the Underground Railroad. To the runaway slaves it was often their last stop before New York, where they could be free. It was also the place where slave hunters could make their last attempts at capture.

I don't know if there ever was anyone named Ivy who escaped slavery thanks to the help of a woman named Franny Butters, but it is *not* fiction that there were people who were opposed to slavery, and they helped many escape via the Underground Railroad. It is also a fact that there was pressure on free citizens to capture escapees; there was even a law requiring it. In spite of the law, good, brave people continued to do the right thing. And I imagine that a lot of their stories are secrets that unfortunately are now lost in time and will never be told.

Recipes from Lay to Rest

Make sure an adult is around when using the stove and knives! These recipes make 4–6 servings.

MRS. O'FLYNN'S OATMEAL

Ingredients:

6 cups apple juice

1 tsp cinnamon

3 cups quick oats

1 cup chopped pears

½ cup maple syrup

½ cup berries

⅓ cup vanilla yogurt

(Chopped nuts optional)

Preparation:

Combine apple juice and cinnamon in a saucepan. Bring to a boil. Stir in oats, chopped pears, syrup, and berries. Reduce heat and cook until most of juice is absorbed, stirring occasionally. Add nuts (if using). Top each bowl with yogurt.

JOYCE'S AMAZING HOT COCOA

Ingredients:

I cup buttermilk (reduced fat)

3 cups milk (skim or I%)

2 cups sweetened condensed milk

¾ cup chocolate syrup

 (more if you like it really chocolatey)

Whipped cream—as much as you want

Shaved chocolate on top—yummy and pretty

Preparation:

In a saucepan heat the buttermilk, milk, and con-densed milk, stirring constantly with a whisk. When warm, add chocolate sauce. Transfer to mugs and top with whipped cream. Sprinkle the whipped cream with chocolate shavings—you'd be crazy not to.

JOHANNA'S CHICKEN SPREAD LUNCH

Ingredients:

I (I0.75 oz) can condensed cream of chicken soup

I envelope (I Tbsp) unflavored gelatin

3 Tbsp water

¾ cup mayonnaise

I (8 oz) package cream cheese, softened

I cup each celery and onion, chopped

I (5 oz) can chicken chunks, drained

Preparation:

In a small pot, heat chicken soup.

In a small bowl, combine gelatin and water and stir it into the heated soup. Blend mayonnaise, cream cheese, onion, and celery into the soup mixture. Add chicken chunks and continue mixing. Refrigerate overnight.

Spread on a toasted English muffin.

Cut in half.

Pack for lunch.

ELLIOTT'S SLOW COOKER MAC AND CHEESE

Ingredients:

12 oz cooked elbow pasta

4 Tbsp unsalted butter

2 (12 oz) cans evaporated milk

2 eggs

I cup milk

⅓ cup flour

4 cups shredded cheddar

    (or 2 cups cheddar and 2 cups mozzarella)

Dashes of salt and pepper

Preparation:

Mix all ingredients in the crock. Cover and cook on low for 3.5–4 hrs, or until pasta is cooked. Don't overcook or it will get mushy gushy.

ROZ'S VERY FIRST EGG SALAD

Ingredients:

8 eggs

½ cup mayonnaise

I Tbsp yellow mustard
    (the sandwich spread, not the spice)

¼ cup chopped green onion

Dashes of salt and pepper

Preparation:

Place eggs in a saucepan and cover with cold water. Bring water to a boil and remove from heat. Cover and let eggs stand in hot water for about 10 minutes. Remove eggs from hot water, cool, peel, and chop.

Place the chopped eggs in a bowl. Stir in the mayonnaise, mustard, and green onion.

Season with salt and pepper.

Stir and serve on bread or crackers.

CREAMY TOMATO SOUP

Ingredients:

2 (15 oz) containers chicken or vegetable broth

1 (28 oz) can concentrated crushed tomatoes

1 cup half-and-half

Dashes of salt and pepper

Cheese for topping (optional)

Preparation:

Combine broth and tomatoes in a medium saucepan over medium heat. When soup bubbles, stir in half-and-half and reduce heat to low. Season with dashes of salt and pepper and simmer for about 15 minutes, stirring continually. Puree soup in a blender—might want to hold blender with an oven mitt.

This is so good if you top with melted cheese: provolone, Asiago, cheddar, Gruyère, Swiss, etc. and serve with crusty bread.

MRS. O'FLYNN'S CRANBERRY-TOMATO CHUTNEY

Ingredients:

5 cups cranberries (fresh or frozen)

1 (16 oz) can crushed tomatoes

I cup raisins
I cup sugar
Dash of salt

Preparation:
Combine all ingredients in saucepan and bring to a boil. Reduce heat; cover and simmer for about 25 minutes, stirring occasionally. Cool. Cover and refrigerate for 2 days before serving.

TOMATO, MOZZARELLA, AND AVOCADO SALAD— FIRST PRIZE WINNER AT THE TOMATO BALL

Ingredients:
4 tomatoes, cubed
3 big balls of fresh mozzarella cheese, cubed
2 soft-ish avocados—peeled, pitted, and cubed
3 Tbsp balsamic vinegar
3 Tbsp red wine vinegar
½ tsp basil—dried or fresh
I tsp sugar
Dashes of salt and pepper

Preparation:

Toss tomatoes, mozzarella, and avocados in a bowl. Mix vinegars, basil, sugar, salt, and pepper in a separate bowl. Pour dressing over salad and mix it up.

You could serve this with crusty bread, toast, or crackers.

ROZ'S VERY FIRST CHICKEN POT PIE

Ingredients:

1 pound cooked chicken breast
2 jars premade turkey or chicken gravy
1 bag frozen mixed vegetables
1 package refrigerator biscuits

Preparation:

Preheat oven to 350°F. Chop chicken into bite-size pieces. In a large mixing bowl mix chicken bites, gravy, and frozen mixed vegetables. Flatten the refrigerator biscuits and line the bottom of a Pyrex dish or ramekins with dough. Bake biscuits for about 8 minutes. Pour the chicken mixture over partially cooked dough and top the mixture with more flattened dough. Bake until biscuits are browned, about 45 minutes.

CORK'S CHICKEN PARMESAN RECIPE

Ingredients:

4 breaded chicken breast cutlets

2 jars store-bought spaghetti sauce

2 Tbsp fresh basil leaves, thinly sliced

1 cup freshly grated Parmesan cheese

8 oz mozzarella cheese, sliced

Preparation:

Preheat oven to 400°F.

Place chicken cutlets in a baking pan. Top with sauce, basil, and cheeses.

Bake until chicken is cooked through, cheese is melted, and sauce is hot and bubbly, about 20 minutes.

Acknowledgments

Sydney Mackenzie Knocks 'Em Dead is what I've heard referred to as a "trunk novel." That is, it was drafted long ago (circa 2008–2009) and put in a trunk for many years before finding its way to editing and publication. Luckily, I still write with the same wonderful group of partners as I did then. So, once again, thank you to Gale, Carolee, Josette, Jane, Chris, and Shannon.

While I would hate to be lost in a tunnel under a haunted cemetery, if I had to bring someone with me, it would be my tireless editor, the wonderful Alyson Heller. This marks the seventh book we've worked on together. Aly, I'm so lucky to have you!

When I think of my tombstone, I imagine it will be alongside the gang who constantly hears about half-baked plots, characters, and settings: Kevin, Ellie, Evan, Happy, and, of course, Mom and Dad.

Most of all, thank you to my readers, the librarians, the teachers, and the parents who read and recommend my books. I hope you love *Sydney Mackenzie Knocks 'Em Dead* as much as *Lost in Hollywood, Lost in Ireland, Lost in Rome, Lost in Paris, Lost in London,* and *Just Add Magic*.

Don't miss another great read from
Cindy Callaghan!

Coming August 2018